OTHER AVENUES

A novel

by
Ann Knight

Blessings!
Ann Knight

This book is a work of fiction. Names and characters are the product of the author's imagination and any resemblance to actual persons, living or dead, is entirely coincidental, with the exception of the late Bishop of California, The Rt. Rev. James A Pike. This characterization of him is, however, fictional.

Canadian Cataloguing in Publication Data

Knight, Ann, 1943–
 Other avenues: a novel

ISBN 0-9695889-4-1

I. Title.

PS8571.N49O83 2000   C813'.54   C00-931677-9
PR9199.3.K54O83 2000

Typesetting & design: JDM ASSOCIATES, Willowdale, ON
Cover design: Willem Hart, Toronto
Printed and bound in Canada

A Kestrel Imprints Novel

from
MONEY JAR Publishing
642 Sheppard Ave. E., Suite 1711
Willowdale, ON
CANADA M2K 1B9
Tel. & fax: (416) 223-7312
E-mail: millyard@home.com

CONTENTS

To
Marianne Williamson,
Kenneth Sylvan Guthrie,
and all, living and dead, who
are building a bridge
from worldly,
dogmatic religion to
the greater spiritual reality,
I dedicate this work.

As we build it, Sophia comes.

OTHER
AVENUES

What Dreams May Come

May 26,1990

//Oh, yes. Mmm." Bliss stirs on her side of the rectory's king-size bed after voicing her ecstasy. The cry hasn't disrupted her sleep.

Dreamtime is a priestly dimension, and the Rev. Bliss Bihar Birch claims each night's joys as enthusiastically as she cherishes the opportunity to step into her pulpit on Sundays. "Mmm." The sleeping woman priest can make out her dream lover's features well enough to know they are *not* those of her husband, Sam Garland. In fact, if she were to consider it, Bliss would discover she's *never* made love to her husband in her dreams. Two priests at play in the garden of nocturnal delights might be one too many.

As if on cue, Sam rolls in the direction of his wife and sleepily drapes an arm over her body. His fingers remember the way. They have teased this nightshirt back from her flesh many times. Even before he realizes he's ready for love, Sam has pressed his naked thighs against the backs of Bliss's bare legs. Gently, he pumps one of her breasts.

"Beeb?" he whispers. "Bliss?"

"Yes!" Her voice is deep and erotic. But *so* loud, Sam goes limp with the realization his wife is still asleep. *Cuckold or a passive voyeur?* Again, his fingers make the decision. *Active voyeur.* He'll pleasure his lady even though he is blocked by the curtain of sleep. At the window, a black Southern California sky flashes white with heat lightning. It's threatening to rain. The idea, *I'm a pretender, threatening to reign,* pushes itself into Sam's brain. It feels like his own thought, and Sam incants it softly—an unbidden mantra of pretense, kingship and proposed power: *I'm a pretender, threatening . . .*

An agreeable kingdom greets him in the collection of photos

atop the dresser. It's an odd array, of clergy friends mostly—poised at ordinations, weddings, baptisms. There's even a colorful funeral procession. One large postcard shows—*Is it Westminster Abbey? St. Paul's? Where is it they conduct coronations?*

Sam Garland is pretty sure he remembers. The stone beneath the coronation seat is the one they say Jacob used as a pillow the night he was visited from above. It's been the object of many an international Capture-the-Flag intrigue. Boyish, if not brutal battles have been waged to secure possession of this particular rock, as if it were the one upon which Christ proposed to build a church. Can the protection extended to an ancient stone pillow tucked beneath a monarch's chair, bleed conscience into the prick of a king? Do a few monuments keep the peace between warring societies? Somehow, after midnight, Sam finds it easier to accept unique takes on human ancestry. Humankind may have had little to say in the beginning. Godlike giants descended from heaven. Yes. According to the Old Testament, they intermarried with earthlings and defined diplomacy. Or defied it. Sam realizes it's a strange thought for a man cradling an orgasmic woman to contemplate. But some things *are* older than sex.

Sam, rector of L.A.'s second-largest Episcopal Church, rides the night and its lightning flashes to a world away. Feeling Bliss's passion, he journeys toward an unwitnessed climax of his own. On a Sunday, standing at his All Souls' pulpit—some twenty miles and possibly that many light-years from Bliss's platform in the barrio—Sam often breathes in the emotion he feels rising in him now: *Though we are apart, yet we are one. We are one.*

Thoughts less noble come on the heels of these good ones: *This isn't the only time you've sacrificed yourself on this woman's altar. A pattern here? Payback for every occasion you took pleasure at another's expense?* Sam knows he couldn't begin to name each person, each woman, he cheated. *You called them your beach bitches! You didn't speak with a civil tongue in those days, Father Garland.* The seasons weren't long enough on the Northern California coast for a good-looking guy who liked to surf to get all the summer satisfaction he could want. But the seductive Sam Garland seldom came up short.

There are worse ways of opening the night than holding the most beautiful woman in the world, Sam thinks as he rolls back to his side of the bed. When James was a baby, Sam endured many sleepless nights with nothing for comfort but the departed spirit of his mentor, San Francisco's bad-boy bishop, James Pike. Sam's family life was in shambles; his promising career as the rising star among Colorado Episcopalians was on the rocks after his failure to win election as their bishop. Many, but especially Bliss, had presumed him capable of being his father-in-law's, Donald Birch, successor. Sam had courted a form of insanity then. Nightly, he reviewed the prospect of laying aside his vocation. Finally, the very day he turned down a respectable university teaching job, the invitation to interview for the All Souls' post came.

"Go back to sleep." Sam hears it clearly.

And sleep returns without another thought. Sam's mentor and guide, the former Bishop Pike, has spoken it.

* * *

Waking, Bliss Birch will reclaim her memories of the night and put them in a mental scrapbook. Pictures made in heaven. Harmless enough by moonlight, but the pageant couldn't play without hazard by day. Too sensually explicit. This dreaming of hers, which began after she was made a priest, seems to be a form of escape. Following in her father's footsteps, Bliss took up the challenge of preaching. And shortly after that, perhaps because Anglicans teach that one isn't held responsible for anything undertaken in a dream, she began to make love in that secret place, to strangers. Custody of this nocturnal scrapbook poses no burden, though Bliss finds that keeping it a secret gets harder.

Sam's private thorns *aren't* private, like his not having anyone who can tell him whether or not his name stands for something. Is Sam short for Samuel or, as Bliss sometimes jokes, Samson? On their first date, Sam told her, "I'm a kite that's broken free. I might crash. But I'll get a glimpse of heaven first." Although she was engaged to someone else, that served as an engraved invitation, "Come, fly with me, Bliss." The conservative bishop's feminist daughter, whose feet had been rooted as long as anyone could remember, could not resist Sam's sky. She still can't. But rather than annoy him with any particulars, she feigns amnesia regarding certain dreams. It's not a territory she documents. There's no bedside dream diary.

Bliss finds Sam more than handsome. He exudes energy. Miraculously, his enthusiasm never exceeds the capacity of those he engages. He's not pushy or gushy. Just friendly. With parishioners, he finds the place that's been carved out for him and fills it without asking for more. One warden likes to play tennis with Sam. Another does lunches. Sam brings several people to his office once a month for a prayer breakfast. Others need telephone time. And Sam is flexible. Except in one area. He asks his friends not to address him as Father.

* * *

It's not even 6 a.m., Saturday, and Sam has said Morning Prayer privately. He's already showered and shaved. As a rule, he showers in the bathroom adjacent to the sauna downstairs. Because Bliss needs more sleep than he does, Sam avoids using the en suite off their bedroom. He'd rather be out of earshot when brushing his teeth. So when the weather is nice, he slips out of their bedroom through the French doors facing the foothills and takes the stairs off the balcony to the pool deck below, coming back in by the sauna entrance. This household is old-fashioned in one respect. They don't lock their doors. The property is doubly fenced, but the pool gate latch is only padlocked when the rectory's occupants are on vacation.

Occasionally after showering, Sam returns immediately to awaken Bliss with familiar gestures, easy talk, and an invitation to sex. But usually, he takes time for himself in the kitchen first. Sitting at the table in the breakfast nook, he writes in his journal. It isn't writing in the usual sense, but rather the recording of dictated impressions from his dead mentor.

This morning, scanning himself in the full-length mirror, dripping dry, Sam tousles the silvering curls on his head with both hands. Lifting a sky blue terry cloth robe from a hook, he wraps himself in it as he heads toward the pantry to put on a tape. From the controls here, stereophonic sound can be channeled to seven units placed throughout the house and yard. Sam designed and installed this "Garland Special" using expensive silver wire and calculating the shortest route to each remote unit. He wanted the sound deterioration kept to a minimum and the integrity of his collection kept at its maximum.

Although a case of canned salmon has lobbied its way onto the lowest shelf in this, his musical storehouse, all the upper cupboards of the pantry are strictly reserved for the albums, cassettes, videos and discs Sam has personally cataloged. The perfection of his system is arcane. Bliss operates it only with his assistance. She carries a boom box to the places where she wants entertainment. After loading a selection, Sam gathers his red notebook from its pantry cabinet file. A rippling brook, "Yosemite, 1965" soon washes the air—one of Sam's homemade nature tapes. Images from that long-ago day when he dreamed of finding a life partner who loved hiking as much as he did dance in his mind like pictures from a *National Geographic* photo essay.

He seats himself at the kitchen table and looks east into the trees, into the portion of an old orange grove he persuaded the developers to leave standing. Almost before Sam can give it his full attention, he has recorded the opening lines of this morning's dictation:

> *We're ready to align the seven and the twelve. The reason I learned flight paths and you memorized Plato and Zecharia Sitchin is clear. We're part of a larger pattern, an amphictyony.*

Sam rereads Pike's strange opening. Seven could represent time or levels of existence. Shakespeare's ages of man. The twelve could stand for space, or relationships. Amphictyony, the relationship between members in a group of twelve? Sam can only recall one other time he's received a word from his mentor that wasn't in his own vocabulary. Sam resumes the dictation. He's a patient secretary:

> *A spiritual Apostleship is in place—always. All ways. Its counterparts, perpetually reconstructed. Look at juries: 12 members. Your vestry: 12 people. The zodiac is an ancient figment of this. We regard it as tragic that mainstream religion has so recently lost touch with sky knowledge. A true priest must not. Scripture warns about losing savor, literally losing one's sense of "the seasons." Astronomy gobbled up astrology without one salty thank you.*
>
> *Plato's ideal city wasn't Jerusalem (with its twelve tribes), but Magnesia—where he believed it was possible to stage no less than 365 festivals a year. That's what you and I do here, Sam. Bless you. We've kept to this discipline nearly 21 years. As your mother would be happy to tell you, "Such faithfulness will be rewarded."*

Sam lays aside his pen.

* * *

Upstairs, Bliss dreams on. "Do you have to leave?" she asks a young English major. He's getting back into his clothes. She knows—in that way which won't make any sense later—that he's an English major because he's using his left hand to blow her kisses.

"I have a Derek Hunter novel to finish for my final exam," he says. And that explains everything. At the mention of the novelist's name, Bliss is transported. She's standing beside a swimming pool. Her own, in fact. She can see California's celebrated author, Derek Hunter, clearly. He's decided to swim—here. Bliss knows without being told that he's going skinny-dipping. He beckons her. Immediately, she is in the pool and sensually entangled with him. The priest in charge of Church of the Ascension feels a profound embarrassment. She looks around to see if anyone is watching. *I'm with Derek Hunter—again?*

* * *

Sam is troubled. He returns the journal to its locked drawer. This morning's closing lines have come off the page and into his belly. *Maybe I'm just on alert because I want to show some of my entries to Andrea*, he thinks. Andrea is his shrink.

"Maybe you're on alert, because I mentioned your mother," Pike counters.

Because of the threat of rain, Sam sticks to the inside passageway, going through the formal dining and living rooms, into the front hall with its walnut staircase, carved banister and the rectory's much-praised antique chandelier. He takes the stairs two at a time. In many respects, the Reverend Sam Garland has done little more this morning than his neighbor has. That man routinely walks the family's dog in the orange grove as Sam settles down to record his guidance from the world of spirit.

At times, Sam has to remind himself he was able to transcribe his "voices" without the orange orchard, that neighbor or his dog in sight. There was a time he put no tape on to hold ambient noise at bay. And, long before that—before Bliss Bihar Birch came into his life—he heard no voices whatsoever.

"Beeb?" he calls her nickname as he tops the stairs.

Sam thinks of his wife as his opposite. She brings light and laughter to an often-dark world. Her childhood was as overprotected as his was unprotected. She has the blessing of a small congregation. Ascension is attended by conscientious academics and liberals who don't consider it burdensome to drive to the heart of the city for Sunday services. All Souls, Rosemead, on the other hand, is a conservative, wealthier and, some would say, notorious, flock of Episcopalians. The fact that Sam's congregation prefers to call itself Anglican is a clue. Ritual, of the high church variety, is cherished. Sam's incubation in two cathedrals at the end of two stellar careers, Pike's in San Francisco and Birch's in Denver, stood him in good stead to lead them.

"Beeb?" Sam calls again. It has the ring of "Babe," the way he says it. At the door, he unties his blue robe and lets it fall open.

Bliss is sitting up in bed, waiting. The frayed edge of her old prayer book pokes from beneath her pillow. She's finished her prayers and is brushing her hair. Stroke. Stroke. Sam takes it in, in slow motion. Stroke. Stroke. *I'd swear you had just made love,* he thinks. She surrenders the hairbrush. He pushes the prayer book onto the bedside table. She slides the pillow from his side of the bed under her knees and he tugs hers aside. He loves the way her shoulder cradles in his arm.

"I love you," he whispers. *And it's so easy to say so.*

Bliss returns her husband's exploratory kisses. But she senses there is something he is bursting to say. She opens her eyes and pushes against his arms. "What? What is it, Sam?"

"I don't know exactly. My angels . . . after all this time . . ." Sam takes a corner of the bedspread and lifts it in front of his mouth, as if he can turn it into a makeshift confessional screen. He so seldom mentions his journal to Bliss that he isn't certain how to pursue this conversation.

"After all this time," she echoes.

Sam straightens up and pushes the bedspread between his thighs. "I'm wondering whether my mother may still be alive."

"But she had a *complete* breakdown when your father died," Bliss says. She can remember only that Sam was "*very* young" when he was abandoned and became a ward of the state. When they were courting, Sam once summarized his sojourn in a series of foster homes as hell. He asked Bliss to let him leave it at that. So she did.

"I had the impression she was dead, but . . ." Sam trails off.

"Maybe there's some way of checking," Bliss suggests. Sam

hears a professional confidence in his wife's tone. It drops him into his terrified gut. *God!* Something robs him of his desire. And that's bad news. Because *she* is ready. *A lady in waiting.*

"I think it's gonna rain," Sam says. He looks out at the foothills and rolls out of bed. Sex play and the morning's conversation have ended.

"Sam? Honey?"

"I'm completely distracted, sorry. But take it from me, Beeb, you had a fabulously good lay in your dreams."

Bliss sighs. "I don't keep a secret so well."

"Neither do I. Sorry." Sam helps her out of bed ceremoniously, as if he were helping her down from a horse-drawn carriage. For a moment, Bliss glimpses a woman like herself, but lifetimes ago. Lady Jewel. She's stepping down to be attended hand and foot. *I didn't expect to fall in love with my father's footman. A literal groom.* Bliss wonders, *Did an ancestor of mine marry beneath herself?*

The bishop's daughter has no sense that *she* married beneath *her*self, so the unbidden thought, and the almost-seen past life vision slips away before she can put her feet in her house slippers. Bliss takes no offense at Sam's reversing his romantic intentions. Savoring the memory of Derek Hunter suits her fine. Sam will have other mornings when he's distracted. That's a given. But dreams of Derek, the only other man she ever slept with *after* marriage, are rare.

2

Emptying the Sky

Later, the same day

I t's nearly midnight. It's the second weekend since Sammy Davis Jr., Jill Ireland and puppeteer Jim Henson died. The Dodgers have won eight of their last eleven games and are in first place. But Magic Johnson, James Worthy and Jerry West are taking heat for not keeping the Lakers in the playoffs.

A downpour of rain hasn't restricted night life. Adult video shops, bars and a massage parlor are open. Two antiquarian bookstores sit in dark isolation on the same block with Church of the Ascension. According to its sign, Bliss Bihar Birch will conduct services here in the morning. However, the only religion being practiced in the neighborhood at this hour professes a "seeing is believing" creed. If it can't be stripped down, it can't be appreciated.

The *Strip*, a portion of L.A.'s famous Sunset Boulevard, snakes through a glittering ghetto ten miles west of here, caretaker to America's Runaway Nation. Kids, learning the price of Easy Money. If you don't write a better contract, Hollywood will help herself. The flashy Movie Capital of the World is capital letters and Technicolor. She taught Las Vegas that appearance counts double. Tinsel Town suckles on the sorrows of her terminally ill celebrities. She finds hope penciled in the margins of bottom-drawer treatments no longer bearing Art Buchwald's, or anyone's, name. Her producers sprinkle enough oversights across a project to keep studio legal departments fully employed.

But this Eastside strip could be called Tequila Sunrise Avenue, Beverly Hills' unnoticed ugly stepsister. There are no Musco lights to suggest one has stumbled onto a movie set. The barrio is capital of nothing in particular. Her boulevards have colorless designations: Mission, Valley, Foothills. Foothills used to be a highway going everywhere. However, no one living near it these days has ever taken it to its end. Truant officers won't work this district after noon. They don't want to be knocking on doors once the drug dealers are awake.

Easy money is the common denominator. It has disciples in all over the city. This is the reality no theatrical revelation can redeem, the underbelly of urban existence. Drug-hungry suburban mothers with a week's grocery money in their wallets frequent this neighborhood. Curious, sex-driven husbands whose sleeping wives are eight-months pregnant, cruise around.

The clouds light up without warning.

The entire sky is as bright as a sunbeam flaring off the crest of a wave. A bolt of lightning scissors out of the heavens. Another. A clap of thunder applauds. Perhaps a future De Mille, lurking on a side street, anticipated his opportunity and captured tonight's sky on celluloid. It would be awesome footage.

Behind Bliss Birch's high altar, off-camera, fire separates Ascension's indigo-colored draperies as easily as Charlton Heston's parting of the Red Sea. Empty choir stalls flood with blinding light. Sheet music on the organ bench combusts. Tomorrow's anthem carries flame across the sanctuary on a gratuitous, invisible wind. A dozen candles, fixed in a dozen brass candlesticks on the concrete rear altar and half a dozen on the new, free-standing walnut communion table, spontaneously flicker alive. They burn for several minutes before melting in the gathering heat.

Seat cushions collect sparks falling from fiery rafters overhead and kindle into flame the cloth on the pews. Prayer books, service leaflets and hymnals ignite. Flowers lovingly selected for the festival high mass at ten in the morning wilt in their vases. Water in a cruet on the credence table comes to a boil, breaking the glass. That tiny pitcher was older than the oldest member of this church. Timbers, above, swallow and nurture the hot gases, recycling them to every part of the roof. Somehow, a portion over the south vestibule entrance is spared as beams and floor joists crackle.

It sounds as if someone is coughing.

From the street, Ascension's stained glass windows glow eerily in the aftermath of the rain. Apostles' faces blink like neon advertisements, alternating between darkness and illumination.

Yet all this combustion goes unnoticed. Neighbors half a block away hear nothing. The fire is unreported in its first twenty minutes.

No one is paying any attention. When a denim-clad figure emerges from the burning structure, no one sees him.

The youthful Mexican-American boy is sporting the colors of a local street gang on the scarf hanging from his back pocket. He closes Ascension's front doors behind himself almost reverently. Looking around, he gallops away to the east, in the direction of the action.

Metal organ pipes sag. Molten puddles of tin trickle into lavatories in the church basement. As wooden pipes collapse, they moan in modes not heard before. In the kitchen beneath the sanctuary, silverware softens and contorts. Fuses begin to sizzle. They pop like Fourth of July firecrackers. The sound is ominous. The destruction, real. Still, no one sounds the alarm. The bars are open and the customers are carrying on inside—dancing, drinking, throwing darts and shooting pool. They come on to each other to assure themselves of the potency of their charms.

Cynics will smile when they read the report, and declare that turnabout is fair play. Churches that ignore society are ignored by it. But few know the story of Ascension, of its century-long tradition of caring. Even some who do, tend to dismiss her parishioners as do-gooders.

The sanctuary floor gives way about 12:45 a.m. Both altars and the remains of the walnut pulpit tumble unceremoniously into the basement. An anonymous passerby with a car phone sounds the alarm. Toilet bowls shatter. Dishes in the kitchen break as cement smashes glowing-red cupboards.

When the firefighters appear, they can save only the vestibule. Everything else is too weakened. Blackened beams will come down; slices of floor balancing charred pews will drop their cargo into the basement pit by turns. Remaining pieces of the exterior walls will have to be pulled down for safety's sake.

But, for now, all of this is frozen like a sculptor's presentation of the valiant Maid of Orleans and her beleaguered troops heading into battle.

.

3

Until We Are Parted

November 1965

*B*ishop Birch, disgruntled by a virtual stranger's requesting for his daughter's hand in marriage over the telephone, passes the receiver quickly to his wife, Betsy.

"Mrs. Birch?" the would-be groom, Michael Cutler, asks.

"Yes."

But losing courage, he says, "I'm putting Bliss on."

"Michael!" Bliss sucks in a deep breath. "Mother. This seems rather sudden, I know. I've mentioned only one date. But a good thing, a very good thing has come over us. And we'd like to make plans. Michael just wanted to do the gentlemanly thing. Will it be a problem?"

"Only if you need an answer tonight," Elizabeth Birch suggests. "It's going on 11:30 here. We were in bed."

"Of course. I'm sorry. So you think papa just needs to wake up to the idea?"

"It's more than that. There's something he's not saying," Betsy confesses. "I saw him with that sometimes nemesis of his, James Pike. It seemed like they were hatching a match."

"When was this?"

"At the last House of Bishops meeting. I got the impression the scheme involves you."

Stanford, where Bliss is studying social work, isn't far from San Francisco, Pike's ecclesiastical base. But she hasn't had a chance to visit Grace Cathedral. The bishop came once and spoke on campus. Short and small, he had a bearing that contradicted his stature. The man's ego strength encompassed everything his eyes took in. He was the opposite of Donald Birch who, although he's a giant at 6 foot 5 inches, hides himself. After seeing Pike, Bliss had no difficulty resolving to stand up into her statuesque self.

"Your father passed over his billfold photo of you, saying he thought you'd be tickled if Pike would make a Phyllis Edwards of you."

"Deacon? You bet," Bliss says. "But, I can't believe papa suggesting that!"

* * *

Five weeks after her engagement to Michael, Bliss accepted an unexpected invitation to a New Year's Eve cocktail party. It came from Bishop James A. Pike's press officer, a young priest, Sam Garland. On meeting Garland, Bliss experienced an overwhelming sense of regret. *Why didn't I save myself for marriage?* Here, in a clergyman of all people, was someone she could desire, not only as a specimen of manliness without peer, but as the one she might conceivably be faithful to forever. He seemed equally smitten.

The power of this first impression, with its surprising passion, fuelled Bliss on a whirlwind and, initially, clandestine course toward Sam.

Bliss and Sam were wed in early May, three weeks before her graduation, and nearly two months before she would have become Mrs. Cutler, the poet's wife. Bishop and Mrs. Birch were seemingly overjoyed to be told of the ceremony just two days before it happened, though they weren't able to be on hand on short notice.

"I'm glad you've met your match," Donald Birch told his daughter. "What God hath put asunder," he joked, referring to her near miss with Michael, whom he dubbed *that knave*, "let no man join together." Bliss felt a deep delight in finally seeing her father as a human being. It was a rite of passage. Like marriage, it signaled, "You're finally grown up."

* * *

Mid-February 1988

The Beverly Hills Hotel ballroom is crowded with Episcopalians, clergy and laity, who have experience and expertise in exercising their influence in the arena of church politics. A faded Valentine's Day decor lends the reception an air of decadent romance. In two weeks, the new bishop of Los Angeles, Charles Sprockett, will be consecrated. This preliminary champagne party was Charles' own idea.

"Our man's made a name for himself already," a lawyer who served on the search committee informs Sam and Bliss. Everyone is passing time, waiting for an opportunity to bend the ear of the bishop-designate. "I ask you, can anything good come out of the Diocese of Rio Grande?"

Sam Garland is content to make small talk with this barrister who, by allusion, would compare Sprockett to Jesus Christ. Bliss would prefer to move closer to the whirlwind gathering around Sprockett himself.

"Good things often come out of nowhere," Sam says. "I was serving as publicist and appointments secretary to the late James Pike, when I coincidentally met Bliss. It was the last day of 1965."

"You knew Bishop Pike? *The* Bishop Pike?" the lawyer asks.

"I could probably have written a decent biography."

"Why didn't you?"

"Long story. Shortly after his death, I came across a piece of art in Denver, a glowing marble statue, maybe twelve feet high. Very striking. It was titled, 'Liberty Looking into the Wind.' The workmanship was superb. The white stone could have been from the same quarry as that was used for the Lincoln Memorial. It shone as if there were a light inside it. The rock fairly rippled. The lady was vigorous, but so was the wind. There was a handwritten card taped beneath the title placard that said, 'This work took my father twenty years to release. Day in and day out we watched him caress Liberty into being.' I realized, in that moment, that I wanted to take twenty years considering the legacy of Bishop Pike. Only then could I do his memory justice."

"So, isn't your twenty years nearly up? I was in junior high when . . ."

"Good Lord," Sam gulps. "Bliss and I are coming up on our twenty-second wedding anniversary. You're right. I've got eighteen months to get cracking."

"Sprockett would make a better subject," the lawyer suggests. "Half the people in this room have never heard of Pike, you know."

* * *

"I'm Bliss Bihar Birch, rector at Church of the Ascension," Bliss says, extending her hand toward Charles Sprockett's. "You're famous in my house for having mentioned our wedding day in *Carry My Bones Up.*"

"Did I?" Sprockett looks as if he's stretching to pick up a gauntlet. "Were you active in the Women's Caucus?" Before she can answer, he says, "No. You're Donald Birch's daughter. Sam Garland's wife. They told me about you."

Bliss is taken aback by the magnitude of Sprockett's self-congratulatory enthusiasm. She turns to push her empty glass under the nose of a loitering waiter. Lamely, and without looking back at him, she says, "They told me about you, too."

Charles appears to consider this a compliment. He lifts his glass and waits for Bliss to lift hers. When she does, the two toast each other. "Ascension!"

"It's an interesting coincidence, don't you think," Bliss says, "that east of Jerusalem they've marked 'The Spot' where Jesus is said to have ascended, and here, we've named the smallest church in the eastern quadrant of the city, Ascension."

"Did you serve your deaconate there?" Charles asks.

"Not entirely. Sam was serving at the cathedral in my father's diocese when I quit social work. I traveled to Cheyenne, Wyoming, twice a month, and studied for my canonical exams by correspondence."

"I served a term on the Board of Examining Chaplains about then," Sprockett confides, hinting that he may be more familiar than she knows with her ability to answer a Church History question.

Bliss nods. Then, for the sake of a few who appear to have an interest in overhearing this conversation, she pushes on. "I took the exams in '72, expecting the Louisville Convention to approve women's ordination as priests the following year."

"Not!" Sprockett says, also delivering the line for the benefit of bystanders.

Bliss shrugs. "Defeat that year took many women deacons by surprise. Wasn't this the twentieth century? Your predecessor finally ordained me in 1977. I'd been deacon-in-charge half-time at Ascension almost a year, by then."

"Was waiting for the Convention's approval in '76 a tough call, since bishops had already broken ranks and begun ordaining without it?"

"Not really. I had a fall back position," Bliss explains. "I'd been assured of ordination in 1977, no matter what. Bishop Spence agreed with those who felt a bishop had the authority to ordain without a new canon, but he wanted to give the General Convention an opportunity to take the initiative and mandate it."

Bliss decides that characterizing herself to the bishop-elect as a moderate isn't inappropriate. Fourteen years ago, she *was*. She didn't lend support then to the Pasadena priest who mobilized voices across the nation to push, successfully, for the new ordination canon that took effect in 1977.

"Your father was willing to put your husband to work, but he wouldn't sponsor you?" Sprockett asks pointedly. He lifts a beneficent arm around Bliss's shoulder. But with the ease of an Indy driver drafting to effect a pass, she turns out from under his paternal embrace.

"Donald Birch is old school," she says. The bishop's arm is at his side again. Bliss leans a bit closer. "So far as I know, my father has yet to say a good word about ordained women."

* * *

Freeway traffic is light on the drive home. "You didn't shake hands with 'our leader,'" Bliss says to Sam with mock horror.

Sam glances at his wife in the passenger seat. "If you've known one bishop, you've known 'em all."

Bliss forgives Sam his disinterest in the Muck E. Muck aspects of clerical life. He was twenty before he ever laid eyes on a bishop. The flamboyant James A. Pike came upon Sam, homeless for the umpteenth time, in 1956. He insisted on Sam's taking a room in his own house. Eight years later when the handsome tenant had graduated from Cal Berkeley and Episcopal Divinity School, the bishop made him a deacon and then a priest in San Francisco. Sam was the envy of classmates who couldn't understand why this seminarian rated a bishop's tutelage and a staff position at Grace Cathedral.

After Pike's dramatic death in a Judean desert in 1969, Sam collected the books and articles written about his life. In 1983, however, he didn't mention to anyone that he could confirm novelist Philip K. Dick's assertion that a departed soul, not unlike Pike's, was reestablishing contact with former associates. He only said Dick's bishop, Timothy Archer, had so many tragic flaws, it was obvious why the writer had cast the story of his death as fiction.

Sam found it easy to forgive the real James Pike his nonfictional infidelities. But he wasn't as quick to dismiss the bishop's inability to accept the lifestyle choice of his namesake son. Psychic Arthur Ford would never have "brought in" young Jim in front of a curious Toronto TV audience, had he not committed suicide to escape, in part, a father's rejection. If Sam Garland had become the son Pike never had, it was because the bishop had gone looking for a straight kid. His being a street kid didn't matter.

"Did you learn anything I should know about 'our glorious leader?'" Sam asks.

"He'll be living at the beach until summer."

"Seriously, what d'ya think?" Sam asks.

"I got no deep sense of him. He's sort of smug. But that could be a mask he's wearing. He's genuinely happy to be caught in the spotlight. Quite a change from our quiet Bill Spence."

"It could go either way," Sam suggests.

"Do you think so?"

"If Sprockett is not wise in the way a bishop should be wise," Sam begins, "at least he'll be able to organize. Even that will be a welcome change from Spence." Sam gives Bliss a we'll-be-okay look.

"I just hope there's something there. Some*one* there."

In his heart of hearts, Sam knows her instincts are good—her intuition, even better. It's what drew them together. She's as crystalline as unpolluted water. It was "The Hope" in her Sam Garland agreed to marry, and vowed to live with "until we are parted by death."

"I hope you're right," he says.

4

To Be or Not To Be the Pope

May 27, 1990: 3 a.m.

A fter two rings, the answering machine picks up. Fire chief
Thompkinson leaves the Reverend Bliss Birch an ominous
message.

* * *

September 1979

"Poppycock!" Sam shouts. He's reading a bishop's memoir while
sunning himself on a Mexican beach. Having packed along every
Pike-related book he owns, he now must keep to a schedule to
reread them during this holiday. It's Sam's way of commemorating
the tenth anniversary of Jim Pike's untimely demise.

The vacation also serves as a distraction. It overlaps the
national triennial gathering of Episcopalians which, this year, is
being held in Denver. It's the wrong time for Birch's unsuccessful
successor to show up there. Bliss's father retired to Florida two
years ago. Although he remains eligible to vote with the House of
Bishops, he's decided to skip this meeting as well. "I'd prefer not
go on record again," he says, "concerning this women's ordination
business." This convention is being asked to authorize "the
regularization" of the holy orders of eleven women who jumped
the gun in Philadelphia in 1974 and were ordained by rebellious
bishops.

"Listen to this bull. I can't believe it." Sam reads two para-
graphs from the memoir aloud to Bliss:

*Pike's life might have eclipsed his life's work. His character
flaws, not inconsiderable, and episcopal missteps, equally grand,
could have taken up so much of our time in ecclesiastical court,*

we would not have proceeded with the ground breaking work Pike himself keenly wanted done.

Having jumped the gun in declaring one of his deaconesses eligible for the priesthood, and foolishly insisting he could legally proceed unilaterally to make a priest of any woman he chose, Pike would have embroiled the Church in a sanctioning process. That could have compromised the chances of many women, and the stability of the Anglican Communion itself, for decades.

"If you want to know what I think," Sam says, though he isn't certain Bliss is following because her face is covered by a sombrero, "I believe Jim would have instigated ordinations sooner—right after the Louisville vote. Nothing would have been compromised. Moderates would have become liberals overnight—filling the vacuum left when liberals became radicals. Your dad would even have made the leap to moderation."

"My dad," Bliss says, lifting the hat, "has only become a moderate in retirement. He denounced James Pike for daring to qualify Phyllis Edwards as a deacon instead of leaving her adrift as a deaconess. He stayed on that bandwagon long after Jim's tragedy in Israel. What makes you think *any* woman, other than his own deacon, would have shown up for an ordination he helped organize? Philadelphia, just as it was, was a godsend. The movement might have fizzled without it."

"*You* would have let Pike ordain you!"

"Not on your life. I let him officiate at my wedding." Then Bliss jokes, "once burned, twice shy."

But Sam isn't finished with his hypothetical scenario. "Bliss, Hong Kong had been ordaining women for two generations. You know you wouldn't have let a gentleman's agreement continue to hamstring the American Church. For heaven's sake . . ."

"What about a gentlewomen's agreement? Does this House of Bishops have any sense? What if the Philadelphia ordinands don't *want* to be regularized? Why must these priests be singled out again? There is nothing incomplete about what was done five years ago. I tell you, if I had had the courage to show up on that Glorious Monday, I certainly would have the guts to claim I've been delivering up the real thing ever since. There's no need, I'd say, for a second wave of good ol' boys to fix me up so I look as good as their good girls do. Get serious. This is doctrinal shit they're trying to shovel up."

"And you pretend not to have been radicalized!" Sam mocks. "And you pretended no disappointment after the first ballot for papa's successor. But Sam, you nearly quit the church!" Without skipping a beat, Sam dons their accent of intimacy, "You oughta know zees, Meesus. I'd rather be working my beezness out of zee Grace Catheedrawl." It's as close as Sam can come to admitting an ambition to follow in his dead mentor's footsteps. He'd prefer to be bishop in San Francisco.

"And, Meester, you oughta know. This lay dee of yours, she steer clear of that Philadelpheeah, becuz she eez so connect with you. She not going to comPROmise where your career, she may lead." Bliss would prefer not to put anything in the way of Sam's success.

"Pass zee tequeela. And zee orange juice, weal ya?"

"Thees sun, she eez keeling us, perhaps, no?"

* * *

Bliss was working part-time in Wyoming when word of the proposed "Glorious Monday" July 29 ordination service shook through Anglican circles with a Richter reading higher than the one in Bihar, India, the day Donald and Elizabeth Birch were married. Knowing his daughter was close to people organizing the outrageous event, Donald formally invited her to his office for a consultation. He asked Bliss to take a seat in *his* chair, behind *his* desk.

"You've wanted to see the world from this vantage, I'm sure," he began. "What we say must never leave this room." Birch proceeded to parade a number of exaugural matters for his daughter's consideration. Seen in his context, the question of the timing of women's ordination receded in import. Local concerns pressed in. Bliss saw the burden that was her father's to carry. She realized that, sadly, he saw himself bearing it alone. By pulling out all the stops, Donald persuaded his daughter to postpone entering the priesthood until it could be done "decently, and in order."

"Associate with this service," he said, "and Betsy and I *will* disown you." He meant disinherit. Bliss believed he would withhold every dollar, as well as the last of any goodwill that might yet exist between them. "And consider, please, what this would do to your mother." Donald wanted any and all complications Betsy might suffer at Bliss's feet. Both knew from experience that Elizabeth

Birch couldn't remain emotionally stable even at the best of times. "I'm going to do it your way, papa. Not for the reason you think." Bliss didn't elaborate. Following the interview, she had to blow her nose. Had she been a victim? Secrets had been confided. Bliss had accessed her father's business. She could hear a youthful Jesus reminding his parents, "Didn't you know I must be about my father's business?" But, Bliss asked herself, had she allowed *her* father to distract her from *The Father's* business?

"I played Holy Communion long before I played the piano. And I played Being-the-Pope before anyone explained to me we weren't Catholic," Bliss had told the Wyoming committee that approved her becoming their first woman deacon.

Elizabeth Birch had expressed motherly concern when young Bliss was discovered dispensing "just pretend" body and blood during semi-reverent play. How could it happen? Neither Betsy nor her daughter had ever witnessed a woman's doing that. To Betsy's consternation, lines of children came out of nowhere and waited beneath the clotheslines in the backyard for Bliss's dubious dispensation—an oyster cracker followed by a sip of Kool-Aid. Flowerpots on the back stoop served to define an altar rail. Occasionally, Bliss appointed assistants, paying no mind to the gender or age of her recruits. A toddler might chirp "the boggy of Queist," shoving a cracker toward a boy twice his size. And, it seemed to make no difference to Beebee whether her communicants knelt or stood.

Elizabeth decided to look the other way. She didn't want to call the game to Donald's attention. Non-confrontation was a habit with her, and Bliss, in time, mistook it for disaffection. "My mother isn't interested in me," became an unspoken tenet of her deepest belief system. Later, she felt certain the pain of that powerful mantra had triggered her connection to the female aspect of God. And she was grateful.

* * *

Elizabeth Birch died suddenly in 1984. Within days of her funeral, Sam Garland began rereading entries from his morning notebooks. Bliss and her mother had not spoken much before Betsy's death, partly because Bliss found her parents' plan to travel to England to protest the consecration of Bishop David Jenkins of Durham distasteful. "At least take a side trip to Stonehenge. Go to

Winchester and see its cathedral and the replica of King Arthur's round table," Bliss had urged them. But her father had insisted stubbornly, "This has nothing to do with being a tourist, Beebee! Can't you understand?"

Bliss had not said, "Think of what it will do to *her*," though she is certain her father's obsession contributed to her mother's death. But she's equally convinced Betsy always chose to nurse her husband's faith, even his most peculiar expressions of it, at the expense of finding her own.

Once in a Lifetime

As usual, Sam is up first. He conducts an early service. "Mass for sun worshippers," he's fond of calling it, waving toward the recreational vehicles crowding the All Souls parking lot.

The flashing light on the answering machine catches his attention as he puts his morning journal away. Moments after hearing the message, he pours himself a coffee and dials the number of one of his deacons.

"Something unexpected has come up here. You'll have to take the 8 o'clock service alone. Are you okay with that? Good. I'll explain later. Thanks."

Sam reaches for Bliss's favorite china plate and spreads a meticulous arrangement of cheese and fruit.

Breaking bad news doesn't come easy, even after years of practice. It is easier, by far, to share gratitude and praise. And Sam is known for having mastered the art of sincere praise. Altar guild members, the children's choir, staff—all feel sincerely appreciated by their rector.

Bliss looked so beautiful this morning as Sam crawled out of what they jokingly call "the driver's side" of the bed. He will let the food speak of beauty, because he must speak the opposite. *She was so tranquil*, he thinks, her breathing rippling the strands of her white-blonde hair as imperceptibly as a wind, which, though arrested by glass, still manages to caress the curtains gently. She was, for all the world, "Liberty Looking into the Wind." *My hope. My rock.*

"You're still here?" Bliss asks, coming into the kitchen for coffee.

"Sit down, Beeb. There's some bad news."

"My dad?"

"No, not that. Thankfully." *Yet.* Sam feels a tiny wave of relief, but it crests on an ocean of pain he's been building the courage to talk with his psychologist Andrea about. His father-in-law's death, and others, as predicted years ago, by Pike.

Bliss didn't hear. "He was fine when we talked yester. . ."

Sam decides to let Chief Thompkinson break the news. The three words "four-alarm fire" cut across Bliss's projections and blank out her thoughts. She collapses into a chair.

"Oh, God. On our Feast Day?"

Sam lifts the fruit plate. Eating Sunday breakfast is forbidden in this house. Twenty-four years ago, the Birch-Garlands (as they briefly called themselves then) agreed to accept the ancient practice of fasting until after Communion. Sam smiles even as Bliss wipes away a tear with the back of her hand. He shoves a slice of apple into his mouth and chomps it noisily. Bliss accepts the distraction and grabs a slice of jalapeno jack cheese. For several moments they stare at each other and stuff their faces with the forbidden fruit, almost laughing as they transform into childlike figures heedless of anything but what is in front of them.

With the youthful innocence of a curate Sam finally says, "Losing a church to fire is a once in a lifetime experience." Thinking an addendum might make the observation encouraging, he adds, "I mean it. Once."

"So, why did it happen to me?"

Sam wants to pull the penumbra of dawn about them as protection. But nothing comes. Bliss has come back to reality with a thud.

"Meet me," she says, "at Casa Maria's for menudo after your service. You can come back to Ascension and see what there is to see on a full stomach. Thanks for this," Bliss says, reaching for a final piece of cheese.

"Okay." Sam feels a twinge. This sense of helplessness has invaded his life before—when others searched for Jim Pike, missing so far away the first week of September 1969, leaving Sam a fragmented memory of the fatherlike man he'd loved; and again, when his baby daughter died, and his son, James, taken. Fatherhood was abruptly scissored out of Sam's scrapbook. When life must proceed without the components one believed were necessary to it, only God knows why. Sam wants to yell an apology: *I lied,*

Beeb. This isn't a once in a lifetime experience.

* * *

"Blanche, may I speak with you?" Sam Garland calls from his office window to a distinguished-looking woman about to enter the church. Blanche Peters, Bishop Sprocket's personal secretary, is a faithful member of Sam's congregation. She changes her course and heads toward the administration wing, her hands thrust deep into the pockets of a rose-colored trench coat. An off-white scarf at the neck matches her shoes.

Sam ushers her into his quarters where he is robing. "Glad to catch you." Sam seems distracted by having to button his stole in place and Blanche offers her assistance. "The bishop may know this," Sam says, "but I want to bring it to your attention. Church of the Ascension went up in flames last night. Apparently a total loss."

Blanche is startled. "Arson?"

"No. Well, they didn't say. The fire marshal didn't suggest that foul play is suspected. We only got word this morning. I haven't seen it, but I gather there will be next to nothing to salvage."

"Bliss must be beside herself."

"I'm going over after our service."

"It *would* have to be Ascension," Blanche says. "No amount of insurance can cover . . . memories. My parents were married at Ascension."

"Is that right?" Sam knows that since her divorce Blanche has lived with her mother, but he's never heard mention of a father. "I appreciate your being on the inside. Knowing we can get the bishop's ear," Sam says.

"When it can be gotten," Blanche answers. The odd tone of her voice is as far as she will go in confiding to her rector something she has discovered the past two years, that there is something vaguely sinister about this bishop's management style compared to the approach of his predecessor. "I'll see that this comes to his attention, of course. But the bishop is taking his family to Palm Springs tonight for a two-night holiday."

"Whatever," Sam pats Blanche's shoulder as she steps out. "Thank you, Blanche."

Throughout his service, Sam feels as if he is in two places at once. The scene in his mind's eye takes his breath away: superimposed on the charred remains of Ascension's timbers are the pages of a calendar that flip month to month—the way time passes in old movies. Black and white. A year passes in this fashion and the same devastation remains. Sam tells himself, it is going to take a long time for Bliss's congregation to heal.

* * *

"Ten years ago . . ." Bliss begins preaching to a weepy group peering into the smoking ruins of their church. They wipe at tears, smudging soot across their cheeks and detailing the path of grief for all to see. People have decided to sit down, cross-legged. What's a ruined Sunday outfit, under these circumstances?

"...on the last two Sundays of May 1980, lava belched from a mountain in Washington state, a mountain a few hundred miles north of here bearing the name, St. Helen. You've seen pictures of the devastation. I've seen souvenir vials of the ash that spewed into the atmosphere on the occasion of Mount St. Helens's eruptions. Helen (the *sainted one* Christians commemorate) was the Roman Emperor Constantine's mother. According to tradition, she discovered the remains of the true cross in Jerusalem at the place of the skull: the town dump. This morning our building passes for Golgotha, the trash heap smoldering just beyond the wall of the city." Bliss wants to put this tragedy in context. Almost any will do. The congregation is poised, quite literally, on the last solid stretch of floor inside the intact front doors.

"Mount St. Helens sits within the Pacific circle of mountain peaks known as the Ring of Fire. If we choose to see this tragedy as the mystery it is, Church of the Ascension has been included in that circle. We are invited to learn a lesson, probably a tough one, from this catastrophic destruction.

"As I was going over my sermon last night, it seemed better than I'd remembered it. I put my thoughts together three months ago for this feast day, before Bishop Sprockett's office canceled his visit. He *was* scheduled to be here for the first time today. If you can imagine. But he's gone to Redlands, and, the terrible irony is, we can see red. How terribly appropriate I find some of what I'd planned to say. Listen, if you will." Bliss picks up her notes:

"Anyone who's been to Ascension twice knows my favorite proverb: 'Perfect love casts out fear.' Today, I'd invite you to hear it this way: The only thing going to hell—is fear. Our fear.

"Yes, you may tell fear to go to hell. Any fear that isn't connected with the respect due the Holy One is doomed. And that is good news.

"Many of us have dipped into fictional and inspirational works produced by a generation of New Age authors. They lend credence to what traditionalists labeled *agrapha*, literature outside the authorized canon. The word 'channeled' is often associated with this form of expression. It purports to be co-authored in some fashion with the channeler often serving only as a secretary to the discarnate force 'coming through' him or her.

"This age certainly calls forth powers of discernment that we have left to authorities in the past. Avoidance has been the official Christian stance to agrapha for almost two millennia. Ninety years ago, an Episcopal priest in Pennsylvania who translated the Greek tale of Apolonius of Tyana (a Jesus-like figure who worked miracles in Greece just *before* the time of Christ), was deposed for twelve years. He earned his living as a high school teacher until he was reinstated. Kenneth Sylvan Guthrie was his name.

"Often the avoided materials (whether from today's New Age writers or from antiquity) introduce saviors and ascended masters. The plural frightens us off. We don't see God working through agents. It's hard to picture the Christ working *through me*. Through you. And what of that word 'ascended?' This parish is named Ascension. And this is the season we agree to remember Christ's having been raised, not simply in a resurrected body, but so completely he is called Master in those dimensions where his reign has commenced.

'We celebrate with Christians everywhere today, a brother who was raised to the throne of All Grace to begin a latter-day reign as an Ascended Master, singular. But how can we anticipate our homecoming, our reunion with him if we stay attached to our fears, to our particular religious leanings and to our most-treasured icons. During this Ascensiontide, let us rise above our attachments, put aside the distractions of having plenty and plenty to think about, and resurrect once again the simplicity of our calling as Christians, to follow Master Jesus—even unto death."

Bliss tucks her sermon into the handbag at her feet. She begins walking among her people. They get to their feet for a hug. As the Peace is passed, a profound silence settles in. Bliss opens a grocery sack and produces a loaf of bread and a bottle of Welch's grape juice.

"May this represent the first of many firsts we're going to share during our recovery," Bliss says, unscrewing the lid on the Welch's. "We have no wine and no wafers today. We're back to basics. As the grains of wheat, once scattered on the hills were gathered into one to become our bread, so may all God's people from all the ends of earth, be gathered into one . . . . St. Augustine said, 'Behold who you are, and become what you see.'"

* * *

Peter White waves cheerily to Sam who pulls into Ascension's tiny parking lot at one o'clock. Bliss and her warden, Peter, are the only ones left surveying the scene.

"These are the times that try the soul," Peter says, coming over to Sam.

"But, we're up to it," Sam nods. The smell has invaded his nostrils, an odor not at all like the pleasant fragrance that lingers after a campfire.

"When I didn't see you at Casa Maria's, I figured you were still here," Sam says, embracing Bliss. "It's awful. A stink like somebody bled to death." Sam draws upon the subliminal memory of his own father's dying from a bleeding ulcer in the kitchen of the family's home high in the hills above Berkeley. He was not quite two when he registered the aromatic signature of death. Although he has no memory of his parents and no love for those who attempted to raise him (using "serial mahogany") before Bishop Pike came along, he occasionally taps the deepest past without realizing it.

"We're not as bad off as we could be," Bliss says. "We'll be able to save four of the stained glass windows."

"A third," Sam calculates cynically.

"We squeezed into the narthex and didn't mind the soot," Peter adds.

"Fifty-five of us." Bliss picks up a rock and tosses it into the rubble that's fallen into the basement. There's a thud as it hits a charred timber. "One more." This one lands with a splash. She smiles. "We've been baptized by fire."

"You seem in good spirits," Sam concedes. "Would you rather go out to Santa Monica, smell the ocean and get seafood at the pier?"

Once in the car, Bliss begins to ramble. "There was a woman from the paper, *The Times*. She interviewed Peter and me. Left just before you came. Said she'd like to sit down again later. *I'm* the stuff of feature articles, she said. I don't think religion is her usual beat. Our sanity in an insane situation surprised her. Maybe she was looking for a falling-to-pieces story.

"Of course, before we could go ahead with anything, we had to parade around the perimeter letting each stark detail sink in. We were kinda like Joshua's warriors circling Jericho, except, after the fall of the wall. At one point I realized we were going clock-wise—from the parking lot into the alley, turning along the side-walk to come back to the front door again. It's so weird the way the front door didn't burn. From the alley, that's where it hits you. Gone. The church is gone. Virtually everything is a heap of wet, blackened bones collapsed into the basement.

"It's the direction of the sun. We were going in the direction of sun. One of the members pointed out that clockwise is the way Plains Indians go when offering a soul to death or when anticipating a birth. Somehow, we stumbled upon the natural ritual that en-compasses grief and anticipation even though nothing of the kind is prescribed in the prayer book."

"You were led," Sam suggests.

"Yes. But it was telling it to the reporter that made it sink in. That was the blessing. Some parish built in the 1870s or '80s now has the oldest rafters in the diocese. A piece of history is gone. And, I can't help thinking there's a connection with this being the anniversary of the eruptions of Mount St. Helens ten years ago. Peter thinks it erupted three times—he's pretty sure, in 1980. I'd read that last Sunday was the ten-year anniversary of its erupting on the new pope's sixtieth birthday. The article noted that it had also blown on the following Sunday. You know me, I pay attention to those 'double helpings' as a sign of prophecy at work."

"Eli-JAH, Eli-SHA," Sam says.

Bliss falls silent. After a couple miles, Sam reaches over and gently pulls at the hairpins in the chignon rolls at the back of Bliss's head. "I know I'm behind the wheel, but . . ."

"You want I should maybe let my hairs down, meester?" The stylized accent Bliss feigns is the tongue the Birch-Garlands invented as newlyweds. They keep it to themselves. It's personal, silly and sensual. It breaks the rules. And helps restore sanity. Good talk. Bliss once put it in a letter to Sam and called it Godde Talk.

"That would be very nice, Meezus," Sam answers. "You weel, I theenk, find a beetch blanket in the backseat. It's an all-purpose blanket good for all purposes. You would consider maybe lying under it with me on the beetch later? If I feeded you?"

Bliss draws out her words like ropes of taffy. "Oh, meester, you feeded me once today already. Is that not enough with the food stuffing?" Bliss has played her part many times. In this game she often takes the name Lay Dee and raises perplexing dilemmas like what to do about "ring around the collared."

Sam picks up his cue. His accent never quite matches hers. "We will make beauteeful muzeek together at my home thees evening, no? You must keep your strength up. A young girl like yourself with the *ass* sets you have, must not let herself get run down."

Bliss breaks into giggles. "I break my butt fighting sexism so that after fifty, I can thrill to being called *girl*? I love you, Sam Garland. And I love knowing how much I love you. I could probably forgive you anything."

6

Now Pitching for the Angels . . .

Gabriel Luna ducks under a strip of yellow caution tape. He
jumps into the pit of debris in the church basement at a point
where a kitchen window he knew how to jimmy used to be.
Shuffling through odds and ends that avalanched into each other,
he finds several items that used to be stacked in Ascension's
cupboards. He has no need of a serving platter. It's misshapen
silverware and crazy, weird stuff that Gabe wants. And because
he doesn't want his mother on his back about filthy blue jeans, he's
planned ahead. He has swimming trunks on underneath. Going
home, he'll stop at a laundromat and sit with a newspaper across
his lap while he washes his jeans. For the moment, they keep this
charcoal grime off his legs.

After finding a roasting pan to hold his collectibles, Gabe
gathers up several more hand-sized items. He's been thinking
about this all morning. Some members of Menudo, his gang, are
out looking for ways to take revenge today. A few who haven't
dropped out of school already are actually studying for exams.
But those tests are three weeks off. Today's 'sposed to be a holiday.
Gabe wants to have a little fun. Right now. Like a hard on. Like
fire. Immediate.

After he's gathered all he can easily carry, Gabriel Luna makes
his way carefully, with his hands above his head holding high a
roasting pan filled with ammo. He finds the concrete steps leading
up to the vestibule. Here Gabe perches himself on the edge and
dangles his legs into the pit where the darkened remains of the
church lie like an unattended corpse—not yet prepared for viewing.
The back of his jeans eat into the soft edges of the charred floor-
boards. That doesn't matter. On a ragged lip of roof above his
head, Gabe notices three seagulls posted like sentries waiting to
announce his secrets to a far-off god. *They can't shit on me from there,*

is all that matters to Gabe.

Absorbed, the boy with the booty doesn't notice when Bliss Birch's car turns into the alley. He pays no attention as she drives through the parking lot and stops her car behind the stubborn piece of narthex wall that now blocks his view; the wall with its intact stained glass window featuring Mary Magdalene and the effort to carry the gospel of Jesus to Southern France, filters the afternoon sun.

Whing. The first crumpled spoon returns to the remains of the drawer from which it came. At least, that's what Gabe decides. *Close enough.* No one from this end would argue his call. Whing. Whing. The birds don't stir as two more pieces of cutlery whiz down the once visible aisle. Success. And again, success. Feeling up to a greater challenge, Gabe reaches for the baseball-sized object he found floating face down in a pail of sooty water. He looks and, yes, he spots the bucket. It's tilted slightly in this direction. *Just the way I left it.*

Bliss is startled to find a young man seated in front of her when she steps into the narthex, and more shocked at what's happening. "That's baby Jesus' head!" she cries as the unthinking pitcher fires a sinking fastball into the carnage beyond them.

"Oh, Missus." Gabriel jumps up. The birds take flight. "You don't work Mondays."

"Usually, I don't. You're right."

"Don't worry," he says pointing to the roasting pan. "I'll put it back where I found it. And everything. All this, back where I found 'em." The boy points to where the baby's head floats. "That's where I found it. I don't need nothing. I'm not taking nothing, just having a little fun." Gabe pulls self-consciously at the perfect crease he ironed down the front of his T-shirt this morning. "Hmm." The nervous gesture puts a path of smoke-colored fingerprints on either side of the fold.

Bliss extends a hand toward the youthful stranger. "I'm Bliss Birch. The rector. People here sometimes call me Sister, or just Bliss."

Gabriel doesn't take her hand. "Yeah. I know." He turns to face the destruction without making eye contact. "Did God do this?" he asks.

"Lightning, we think. During Saturday's thunderstorm."

"From God?" he asks again.

"Do you think God would destroy a church?"

"Well, I don't know. I'm asking," Gabriel says insistently.

"That," Bliss says with a streak of stubbornness equal to her inquisitor's, "is a question we would need to ask God."

"He'd answer?"

"Oh, yes," she assures the intruder. "But when you ask, you have to have ears to listen for the answer. That's especially true when you're waiting for an answer to a question as tough as that. Don't you think?"

"You'd know."

"What makes you say that?"

There's almost contempt in young Luna's tone. "You're religious," he says. It's not her being religious that he's taking exception to, but the fact that it's been necessary for him to point it out.

"You must be religious yourself. You came here," Bliss says as she considers, *Who are you? Are you dangerous? Should I just excuse myself and wait for the fire marshal outside?*

"I wanted to see what'd happened. Sure smells bad, don't it?"

"It does. The fire department says it may smell this way for another ten days unless we get more rain. And you know what they say about rain in Southern California in the summertime." Bliss then realizes she's alluding to music of another generation. But rather than explain, she asks, "Is that the *only* reason you came, to see what'd happened?"

"Usually I come when things are slow. I'm kinda in the habit now, I guess," Gabriel answers.

"I haven't seen you here before." Bliss looks closely at the Mexican-American boy in front of her. Almost a man. Seventeen, maybe. Big, but not fat. His eyes sag onto brown cheeks that expand across a broad face. Although he won't look at her while she's looking at him, she knows he's already taken her measure. She decides to speak to him in Spanish. To ask about his faith. She's barely finished a question when he begins answering her in rapid English.

"I'm not religious, no. But I got a few questions. Things I wonder about sometimes, ya know. That's all."

"Like, 'Did God burn down this church?'"

"For one. I mean, could He? Would He?"

"Could God create the universe? Could God love *everything* once it was made?" Bliss pauses. "I'm sorry, I'm avoiding your question. I don't even know your name."

"Oh. I'm Gabe. Gabriel Luna."

"Luna. What a lovely name." Bliss wants to reach out and lift his chin, but she doesn't. She can see he's been brought up to respect his elders by diverting his eyes. It would embarrass him to be treated as an equal by her. "You know, Gabe, you don't have to be religious to ask questions about God. It's once you have gotten a few answers, you discover whether you need to be religious or not. Like with drugs." *Where did that come from?* Bliss wonders.

"What d'ya mean?"

"Well, some are habit forming. But not all habits are bad for you. Talking to God, for instance, can be a habit. A good one. Like the habit of letting yourself into the church once in a while. That's good."

"I ain't done so much talking to God. Not like you priests."

"Maybe watching priests you got the idea you didn't need to ask God about things yourself. But you do. You *always* have to ask the important questions yourself. I'd also like to know if God sent us this fire," Bliss says.

Gabriel can tell she's sincere.

Bliss pushes her luck. "What do you think?"

"It don't sound right," Gabe says. "Why would God do something like that?"

"As a lesson, maybe. So we can go ahead and build a twenty-first century church here." Bliss is afraid her reference to drugs may have been too invasive. But she feels that to be true to her calling she must let a kid off the streets know she isn't afraid to talk about life's real problems. *Let the moment unfold itself,* she hears. And dear old Professor Wingate comes to mind. Everyone at the seminary learned some version of The Wingate Injunction, "Don't cram it all into the first open suitcase. No one packs for the Christian Life never to return to the closet." Young Mr. Luna has other questions. He won't ask them all today. *Even if I never see him again, I have to focus on where he's coming from right now.*

Gabe asks, "D'ya think there's a lesson in it for me?"

"That's the question you could put to God. 'God,' you could say, 'is there something I can learn from this fire?' Could you do that?"

Gabriel sits back down. He reaches into his stockpile of am-munition and pulls out a misshapen table knife. "I'd have to come here?" he asks.

Bliss elects to sit down beside him. "Heavens, no. God will listen to you anywhere." She doesn't dangle her legs in the pit, but she's close enough to hear Gabriel's breathing. "Once the line is open, it's kinda like a phone, you can talk with God anytime. Two-way. Like this conversation we're having. Have you tried that?"

"With God? Once maybe, that I know of, I guess," Gabe says. He glances her way and she catches a flash from his dark eyes. He quickly hangs his head. He doesn't want to explain.

"You're one up on a lot of people, then, Gabe."

Bliss realizes the boy doesn't want to go any deeper. Not today. "Once maybe, that I know of" is all the confession he cares to make. And Bliss rests. She's certain this neighborhood Moonchild, Luna, is not entirely ignorant of the spiritual matters he would like to pursue. She leans behind him and reaches into the roasting pan herself. Finding a serving spoon bent double, she asks, "Where does this belong?"

"I'll show you." Gabe lets his knife fly. There's a clang of metal on metal as it lands. "There."

"Whoa. I'm impressed. What'll you give me if I can get this into that bucket with the head of Baby Jesus?" Bliss wriggles the spoon in her fingers.

Gabriel pulls a pair of infant legs out of the roasting pan. "The feet?" he asks. Both laugh. The legs have melted together at the groin. Stringy globules of synthetic material now sit where sex organs might appear on an anatomically correct Baby Jesus. "Kinda gross, huh?"

"I probably can't hit the bucket anyway," Bliss chuckles.

"Want me to show you?"

"Sure." Bliss points to the grotesque legs, "with those."

"Okay. Here we go." But Gabe's trajectory is low. His hit dumps the bucket's contents into the muck all around it. He shrugs. Standing, he offers his hand to help Bliss to her feet. "Well, thank you, Missus," he says in farewell although she doesn't stand.

"You don't have to go. That's only your first miss."

"I should leave. I gotta clean myself up before I go home." He picks up the roasting pan, but drops two spoons on the floor beside Bliss. Then he disappears down the vestibule steps and emerges scrambling over the rubble with the roasting pan held overhead. "See ya," he calls, putting the pan, still brimming with ammo, back where he found it.

"See ya," Bliss calls. *See ya, Gabriel Luna.*

As he shuffles off down the alley, Bliss becomes persuaded of an irrational idea. Had it not been for the fire, this particular boy would have been numbered in the body count, the almost invisible death toll that local gang wars are tallying up. She can't explain the sudden affinity she's feeling for him, this Angel, Gabriel, of the Moon. She is certain he is a boy who has courted danger. She would bet on it.

Everything is good.

Why, then, does so much in this world seem sinister?

Ponder it, in your heart.

So Bliss Bihar Birch, Missus Earthquake, holds to herself all she knows about barrio life in East Los Angeles. It is too much.

I will give you rest.

7

Confession Is Good for the Soul

Monday, May 28, 1990: evening

"It's never too late for a mid-life crisis," Sam told Bliss when he
decided to begin seeing a psychologist last fall. Every Monday
night, he consults Andrea Marvin to talk about his issues. Initially,
he wanted a fresh perspective on his work. He reluctantly admitted
by Christmas that "a few things about my childhood—unresolved
tensions—need attention."

Since Easter, Sam's been considering using his weekly session
for something else, a guided adventure into the strangest topics
covered by Pike in his morning dictations. Predictions Pike put in
writing fourteen years ago began coming true Easter Sunday when
Greta Garbo died.

"It's time I look at *all* the reasons I need Andrea's help," is all
Sam told Bliss last Tuesday when she found him rummaging
through the journals ordinarily locked away in his pantry filing
cabinet. "I'm looking for something appropriate to introduce her
to this discipline of mine. It's odd, isn't it? Your father was my
spiritual director for twelve years and I never once told him about
these. I'd just nod when he inquired about daily prayers. Never
explained any of this to him. Had no explanation myself."

"Protract your mid-life crisis at least until you can harvest its
benefits," Bliss offered.

Sam had gotten up and kissed his wife on the nose, then.
"Bless your heart for not being nosy. I love you."

Until Sam experienced the freeing effect of the doctor-patient
privilege, he couldn't imagine revealing *anything* from his daily
transcriptions. In his experience at All Souls, the confessional is a
place where only diehard traditionalists and a few Catholic
converts come. They request the Sacrament of Penance. Sam

regards their confessions—sometimes lengthy litanies of "all my sins"—as words heard, but *not* heard. He programs himself to forget them. Absolution works in part, Sam supposes, because of this induced amnesia.

But cast in the role of the penitent, in therapy, Sam sees it another way. When Dr. Marvin plays the priestly role, there is a refreshing reversal. And, to his surprise, he finds himself hoping she *won't* dismiss everything he shares with her.

Andrea Marvin is standing beside her open door and motions Sam in. There's no receptionist tonight and Andrea is even working the phones. "Because of Memorial Day," she explains, excusing herself to the outer office to make a new message for the answering machine.

Dr. Marvin feels she and her clergyman client have experienced breakthroughs in the last six months in the areas of clinical language and its applications in describing dysfunction. And Sam feels he's become more cooperative with his therapist, agreeing to let things from his past come forward to inform the present. Rather than maintaining his former go-it-alone attitude where his own troubles are concerned, Sam is now opening to the suggestion that one can make a smoother transition to self-awareness with the assistance of a professional counselor.

Sam sits tapping one knee with the edge of the large paper-sized envelope he's brought along. It contains copies of sample pages from his precious notebooks. Sam notices that he's keeping time with a tiny bird song coming from beneath a draped cage in the corner of the room. *Effie doesn't usually sing once she's been put to bed.* The song doesn't annoy him, but his nostrils flare, assaulted by the smell of bird droppings.

A consultant selected tones of apricot, gray and mint green for Andrea's office. Although its purpose is lost on Sam, the subliminal effect works just the same. He feels totally relaxed here without crediting the gray carpet or apricot-colored walls.

"Do you like my new paisley pillows?" Andrea asks as she sets one aside to sit down.

"I hadn't noticed," Sam confesses. "But I wonder if your cleaning woman forgot Effie?" He nods in the direction of the tea towel–draped cage.

"Goodness. I do Effie myself," Andrea says, getting up. She is a lithe, even willowy woman in her late thirties, Sam guesses.

She is almost too thin, but her face is not drawn or angular. It has a little girl freshness about it that almost contradicts Andrea's mellow voice. "You're right. I've neglected her terribly."

Sam waits as Andrea puts Effie's dirty paper in the trash.

"Go ahead. I'm listening," Andrea says returning to her chair.

"If what I've brought you gets out," Sam begins, lifting the envelope, "I'm in ecclesiastical hot water. I've been locking my morning notebooks away for twenty years. Bliss doesn't even read them."

"Why is that?"

"Certain things, once you know them, or even know *about* them, there's no turning back. I've glimpsed things. Things unseen. But I haven't got a clue how to move forward, having seen them. Which leaves me where I am," Sam confesses.

"And where's that?"

"Limbo. And I don't mean the dance."

"What's that like?"

"Suppose the theory of relativity had been confirmed by a third-century seeker in which it was somehow confided. Would his name have been Einstein? Was that body of knowledge preordained for him to imagine?"

"Does it matter?" Andrea asks. She reaches to pick up some pages of the *L.A. Times* sitting on the gray coffee table between them and begins folding them as she walks toward the bird cage.

"Could relativity have meant anything to an Einstein in a baking sheet universe and one that had never seen a modern baking sheet, for that matter?"

"What are you getting at, Sam?" Andrea sounds irritated. Effie is hampering her effort to reattach the bottom of the cage.

"I realize I'm not simply after *your* 'ear' in this. I want to be able to share my secrets with Bliss, especially now." Sam picks up the paper Andrea left behind. "Did you see the story?"

"The story?"

"You left the second page of it here." Sam begins reading aloud, and Andrea gives him her full attention:

> "*In time, we may understand why we are called to bear this burden,*" *Birch told her parishioners.* "*It isn't necessary to attribute divine intent to a catastrophe. But a catastrophe can shed light upon divine intent.*" *The Rev. Bliss Birch has been serving East L.A.'s Church of the Ascension since 1978. Her*

*church, the smaller of two parishes located in the district, was the
oldest Episcopal structure in Southern California. According to
Warden Peter White it may be weeks before damages can be
assessed. The church is insured under a group policy, he told the
L.A. Times. Diocesan bishop, the Rt. Rev. Charles Sprockett,
who conducted confirmation services in San Bernardino and
Redlands Sunday, could not be reached for comment.*

"What do *you* need, Sam?" Andrea asks. Her firm, caring
question brings a tear to his eyes. She isn't going to let Bliss's
troubles distract her from her job.

"I need help. Getting-out-of-limbo help. There's something
here," he strokes the package in his lap, "I really don't understand."

Andrea leans forward. "The envelope, please."

As she begins leafing through the pages, Sam says, "It's the
page with a column labeled Sunday, Year Eleven Departures, that
I want you to notice."

"This? The Eagle / Serpent chariot?" She hands the page across
to Sam. It lists Ryan White, Greta Garbo, Tony Conigliaro, Leonard
Bernstein, Ray Goulding, Bill Cullen, Hank Gathers, Brian Watkins,
the Rt. Rev. Donald Birch, Church of the Ascension, and Aaron
Copland. "Leonard Bernstein's alive. But aren't most of these other
people dead?"

"Yes, but only recently so," Sam says. "I received this list in
a morning meditation in 1976, before we moved to California. I
only thought of it again this year—after Greta Garbo died."

"On Easter," Andrea says. "A Sunday. But what's the number
eleven about? Sunday, Year Eleven?"

"Well, this year, 1990, follows what Pike calls the eleventh
calendar pattern. There are fourteen calendar patterns and he
assigns them to the tribes of Israel. January 1st can fall on any of
the seven days of the week and the seven leap year patterns create
another seven variations. Fourteen in all."

"I've never given it any thought."

"Neither had I," Sam says. "This particular piece of dictation
conveys departures information for those leaving on the Sunday,
Eleven chariot. My father-in-law is there; maybe you could say,
he's *scheduled* to leave life on this chariot. That's troubling. But we
also have the arrivals list for the Eagle / Serpent chariot. That drew
my attention to the fact that Lena Horne and Buddy Rich had been

born on the same day."

"A Sunday?" Andrea is trying to comprehend.

"Yes. And, it's true. They were born on the same day."

"But none of this is what concerns you," Andrea says with conviction.

"No. What concerns me," Sam says, "is the coincidence factor. I pulled this page from my old notebook last Tuesday and copied it to share with you tonight. At midnight Saturday, first thing Sunday, Bliss's church—which is right there on the list, for God's sake—began burning. I mean, this is more than a smoking gun. It's an invitation to understand that after his death Bishop Pike had the power to access the secrets of life and death."

"Pike is the one you believe 'sent' this information to you in 1976?" Andrea asks.

"I *know* it was Jim. As clear as I'd recognize the voice of someone on the phone."

Andrea looks at something else Pike said:

> *Have you forgotten the reason I am instructing you concerning time, and the purpose of coincidence? Arrivals and departures attract spectators. There's a spiritual need at the root of the persistent human attraction to seemingly irrelevant information. My body was found on September 7, 1969, a pattern seven calendar. That Sunday has a recognizable signature. Each chariot, if you can understand it, is a flame. We resurrect with consciousness intact. We are alive.*

Sam had replied to this assertion with questions:

> *What is the point of compounding psychic information? Aren't answers to prayer sufficient? I'm left here with fifty-two possible death dates for my father-in-law in any Number Eleven (tribe of Asher) year: 1979, 1990, 2001. And, again, if he should live so long, 2007. This isn't something I can share with anyone. Not even* Bliss. *It may seem concrete to you, but is it real?*

Pike had responded:

> *You'd prefer I carve it in stone for you! You will share it. But take your time. That's what other-worldly communication teaches:* accomplish what is within you to accomplish, *at your preferred pace. You'll discover, Sam, what you have in common with all seeds—borne for a time on the wind, they fall. Grounded, they are dependent upon the ingredients of divine metamorphosis. The Eagle/Serpent chariot has carried landscape*

artists to new landscapes. Two Hall of Fame ballplayers caught this particular vehicle. The ego drops off like a snake skin. Life and lifetime are not synonymous. When you are ready, you may choose to remember other avenues you've strolled upon.

Andrea takes a deep breath and leans back into her chair. "You've had much more on your mind than you've let on, Mr. Preacher Man. The knowledge of life after death. Seems pretty concrete."

"It didn't see this as a hit list when I transcribed it. And there's no reason to suppose Pike and his afterlife associates are 100% accurate. I remind myself that psychic predictions miss the mark as often as not. We probably exaggerate the successes. Exodus claims six hundred thousand people left Egypt and survived forty years in the desert. That's gotta be hyperbole. Jim didn't last but a couple of days in that heat."

"Do you tell your congregation the Bible exaggerates?"

"Not so bluntly. I might say, 'that's the equivalent of everyone between here and Covina packing up what they can and leaving for Las Vegas through the desert on foot, avoiding the highways. Drag that out forty years and make the Colorado River our Red Sea. Is there someone who knows the engineers at the dam so we can cross on dry land?'"

"So, how does this interaction with Pike affect you?"

"It's like taking a good book off the shelf. His morning messages keep me from viewing life in isolation. Like a good book, it connects me with a larger world." Sam pauses and Andrea simply waits. "Death. It isn't as final as we thought. More like a signature at the bottom of a letter. Almost a promise that more letters will follow. Of course, death is a blow. But I hadn't even stopped to notice how profound Pike's 'letters' had been, until the death of Garbo. Easter was when I first understood that the unseen energies aren't so much speaking *to* me as *through* me. We're a team. And it's all beginning to get to the people I preach to." Sam slaps his right fist into his other palm and rolls it around like a giant ball and socket. "That's moderately overwhelming."

"Because . . ."

"What does being that kind of team player mean?" Sam asks.

"It means there's genuine power in you. It asks if you're ready to rise to the challenge of expressing your power."

"If I *am* saying that, what does it mean?"

Andrea smiles. "It means I can help."

You sure know how to get along with a woman who isn't afraid of making the first move, Sam's inner bedeviller whispers.

"You're smiling," Andrea says.

"Am I?" Sam picks up the newspaper. He needs to bail out for a moment. "Look at this." Appearing above an advertisement on the page opposite the Ascension fire story is a short piece selected by a smirking editor, no doubt. "Feeding the Flames" is datelined Burlingame. A Seventh Day Adventist minister is under arrest after confessing that he set fire to his church to collect the insurance proceeds. He intended to use the money for renovations. The loss, estimated at a million dollars, completely destroyed the 55-year-old house of worship. The minister admits he blundered; he wanted to torch only a portion of the building.

Andrea dutifully takes the paper from Sam and scans the article. Then she gives it back to him. "Go on."

"What's the purpose of Pike's putting this departures information on the table?" Sam asks. "Is it important that his foreknowledge be acknowledged? Is it as simple as that? He wants it known that the energy he was still commands its intellect, still can attract attention and come through . . . with the goods?"

"So, this is a matter of courage?" Andrea asks. "Of your finding the courage to say, 'He comes through me,' to someone who might not proceed as methodically as we will do here?"

8

Turf Wars and Time Lags

The answering machine has recorded Donald Birch's belabored breaths. "You're not home?" An audible exhale after the observation is a signature all its own.

Bliss's gut responds. *He's disappointed and it's undoubtedly my fault.* Her father's innuendo has been able to bait a guilt trap for fifty-four years, four months and thirteen days now. But who's counting?

"An item on our late news . . . about the killings in L.A. over the holiday weekend . . . ended with a picture of a burned-out church." Donald sighs again. "I thought it looked like yours, Beebee. But,"—exhale,—"you would have called, no? You know we lost two churches to fire while I was in Denver. It can be messy . . . getting a settlement that allows you to replace what you've lost. No need to go into it . . . if you aren't affected, of course." He almost groans, "Give me a call if you are. It's after eleven here. Guess it'll be too late for you to call tonight when you get in. In the morning, okay? One way or the other. I'd be curious to know what church it is, if it *isn't* Ascension. Bye, bye. This is dad." After another sigh he adds, "In Florida, of course."

* * *

Tuesday, May 29, 1990

Blanche Peters usually arrives at diocesan headquarters in the heart of Los Angeles by 8:55 a.m., bringing along a newspaper she's purchased for the bishop. The vending machine is near her bus stop.

But today, it's yesterday's paper she chooses to leave open on Charles Sprockett's desk. Blanche places a silver pen as a pointer beside the photo of the blackened remains of Church of the Ascension. She considered leaving a phone message Sunday, but decided against breaking her pledge not to take her work home. If someone closer to the disaster saw fit, they may have gotten through to him. She promised her rector she'd bring it to Sprockett's attention, but she didn't specify when.

This ability to keep pressure off the one at the top helped land Blanche Peters her in-house promotion two years ago when Sprockett came aboard. "Aboard" is his term. The bishop is inordinately fond of nautical language. So much so, bets are placed in some quarters as to when he'll preach without mentioning the sea. Blanche suspects she might have preferred working for Sprockett's congenial predecessor. William Spence's sudden death three years short of a well-deserved retirement hit the diocese hard. Especially the staff. His secretary took early retirement. Even though Blanche fantasizes how her job might be different with Spence, she knows her temperament is well-suited to the businesslike approach Sprockett prefers. At sixty-one, Blanche never lets her guard down. After thirty years of living on her own, she is back at home tending her elderly mother. She views it as a payback, the consequence of having made a bad marriage and, as she regularly confesses to Sam Garland, "having done those things I ought not to have done."

Serving under a "captain" like Sprockett—who just came in at 10:45 a.m. and grunted in her direction in passing—is part of her penance. One day he treats you like a confidante and the next like a scullery maid. But fair wind or foul, Blanche is determinedly professional. She imagines that she's learned what it is parish priests must absorb, things that bring heartache but that no one expects you to take personally.

"Blanche?" It's Charles on the intercom at 10:55 a.m. "Put in a call to the Church Insurance Corporation, will you? Thanks."

There it is again, Blanche thinks. Spence would have called the rector of Ascension first. Sprockett has it the other way around.

* * *

Three weeks later, Bliss takes up the gavel to chair the June meeting of her vestry at Peter White's home. She has disturbing news to deliver regarding site clean-up delays. The bishop and his Urban Missioner, Deacon Elizabeth Sparks, have not yet visited the site. They're expected at 10 a.m. tomorrow, but they've canceled two previous appointments, so it is anybody's guess as to whether the third time will be the charm.

Bliss explains. "The bishop hasn't spoken with me personally yet, and hasn't returned my calls. My dad, on the other hand, has been phoning twice a week."

Sam assured his father-in-law that Bliss could take the situation in hand without the intervention Donald offered. "It does look as if he's deliberately pushing her back in this situation," Sam agreed. "But you know, Bliss earned her nickname, the Blonde Bombshell. When the peaceable kingdom is ushered in, the lions and the bombshells will lie down together. And those bombshells won't just survive, they'll thrive."

"How do you live with that?" Donald had asked Sam.

"I proved as a youngster I could live with *anybody*," Sam heard himself say. "It was when I finally found someone I didn't want to live with*out* that I had to consider taking this marriage vow business seriously."

"Do young people still get married?" Donald asked in all seriousness.

* * *

Received June 29, 1990

THE DIOCESE OF LOS ANGELES
Office of the Bishop
The Rt. Rev. Charles Sprockett, D.D.

June 27, 1990

Dear Friends,

All of us share the pain of the loss of your lovely sanctuary. It is a tragedy touching many, and our prayers are with you. The courage and faith you've displayed this past month is an inspiration. But with every cloud there is, of course, a silver lining. We're presented with a tremendous opportunity here if we can but see it as such. This fire leaves us free to examine the future of your congregation without the constraints of an attachment to a particular site.

If the best way to keep an Episcopal presence in the East End is by rebuilding Ascension exactly where it's been, I'll endorse that decision. But other avenues suggest themselves, and we must explore them with courage.

I'm entrusted to act on behalf of Episcopalians throughout this diocese. I can't ignore an overall strategy for the sake of a single congregation. The East End is vital to our work, and until this fire, Ascension was vital in the East End. I've asked our Urban Deacon, the Rev. Elizabeth Sparks, to work with you in this matter as you explore your options. She and I visited the site with your rector this past week. If you want my thoughts in greater detail, I'll be happy to meet with your duly-elected representatives.

        +Charles
        Los Angeles

* * *

Sent June 29, 1990

CHURCH OF THE ASCENSION
Spreading the Gospel since 1863

June 29, 1990

Dear Bishop Sprockett,

I'm grateful for the prayers extended in your letter of the 27th. It's helpful to remember that you appreciate the years of faithfulness contributed by members of Ascension parish. Yes, there's a silver lining here, and we have many things to evaluate before we approach rebuilding. Those charged with gathering data about our financial picture as we undertake a decision will doubtless ask for further input regarding the avenues you and Deacon Sparks would advocate.

As I mentioned during your visit, many at Ascension feel the loss of this building keenly because it was the first Episcopal Church in this neighborhood, and because it was in operation even before the Diocese of Los Angeles was founded. I will remain sensitive to the concerns of my congregation, as well as to the sentiments of others who make a regular contribution to our work although they don't worship here.

On Sunday we hold our annual Sunday School picnic, and I'll share your letter with the congregation. God bless you, Bishop Sprockett, and those you love.

Yours in Christ,
Bliss Bihar Birch

* * *

Sunday, July 1, 1990

A tremendous sneeze goes up from an unseen sneezer in the basement rubble. It punctuates the pause at the end of the third stanza of the last hymn, "Christ Is Made The Sure Foundation." The Ascension congregation catches its breath and takes up, "Laud and honor, God Almighty, laud and honor . . . "

Peter White excuses himself. He makes his way in the direction of the sneeze. The basement is still overflowing with debris. Ascension's insurer, CIC, has been courteous in returning calls, but they haven't dispatched an inspector to the site as yet and won't authorize a full cleanup until that initial paperwork is on file. This hasn't prevented a few parishioners from initiating a tidying-up campaign. They come to worship bringing garbage bags and carry home some of the most intriguing refuse: bits of stained glass, scorched prayer books, scrap metal. Bliss told Peter the trash was most likely getting "the relic treatment" once home. She imagines little altars brimming with Ascension souvenirs.

At the bottom of the steps, White comes upon the slumped-over body of a teenage boy. The left sleeve of his sweatshirt is soaked with blood and his cheek is smeared with red-brown dried blood.

"Excuse me," Peter begins tentatively. When the boy doesn't rouse, Peter takes him by both shoulders and lifts gently.

"Huh?"

"Have you been hurt? Do you know where you are?" Peter asks.

Upstairs, patio chairs are being folded up. Feet scuffle and people begin talking. They have a picnic to set up. Other years, Ascension has gone a few blocks away to a city park for this function. But, feeling protective of their habitat, perhaps, this year they've elected to stage the event in the parking lot—even though that meant everyone had to find parking on the street. That isn't so hard to do on a Sunday.

After greeting worshippers, Bliss comes down the steps. "Gabriel," she says in surprise.

"He appears to be hurt," Peter says. "You know him?"

"We've met. Gabriel Luna."

"Menudo's colors." Peter points out the distinctive scarf.

"I maybe just passed out," Gabe says trying to get up, "or fell asleep, I mean." He doesn't appear to have his bearings. "Oh, Missus. Are you ready for church? I should go."

"We need to get that arm looked at. Were you *shot* ?" Bliss asks. She can't determine the extent of the injury, but there appears to be a lot of blood on Gabe's clothing. "You've been losing blood."

"Turf trouble. Yeh. I don't carry no guns myself. Maybe, after this . . . " He doesn't continue. It wouldn't be right to lie to the Sister. The Sister. She said he could call her that. But she ain't nothing like a nun. And, being so beautiful, she doesn't seem old either; even though, Gabe figures, she's older than his mother. Still, it's easy to think of her *like* a sister.

"Let me take you over to County Hospital emergency," Peter volunteers. "They'll fix you right up."

"What do you think?" Gabriel asks Bliss. There's a cornered, wounded-animal look in his eyes.

"Mr. White has a fine idea. I would take him up on it." Bliss is unclear why the boy has left the decision to her. But she's glad he is willing to accept help. Gabe doesn't want any actual assistance getting upstairs, so she and Peter lead. He follows them to the curb and gets into Peter's car as Peter goes around to the driver's side.

Before opening his door, Peter asks, "*Do* you know him?"

"We met once." Her tone suggests caution.

"Wouldn't surprise me," Peter lowers his voice, "if he isn't our local drug dealer. Should I recruit him for the building committee? Those guys supposedly make good money." Peter laughs. He doesn't want a response. He opens his door. "I'll see you at the ball field once I get Gabriel here attended to."

"I'll get you fellas a sandwich," Bliss says.

"No. There's a Kentucky Fried right on our way," Peter says.

* * *

"Do you come to the church often?" Peter asks.

He and Gabriel have made a lot of small talk. They're busy polishing off fried chicken dinners while parked in the KFC lot.

"I've never come to a service, if that's what you mean,"

Gabe says.

"I mean, do you meet your friends there?" Peter insists upon catching the boy's eye whenever he can.

"No. I do my business up the street," Gabe answers. "Is that what you mean?" He returns Peter's steady gaze.

"I'm not sure. We both know this is just a flesh wound and there's no way you're gonna let me take you to the hospital."

"That's true." Gabe smiles.

"So, why did you come this far?"

"For one thing, and I mean this. I really want to know why your church burned down."

Peter shakes his head. He'd assumed things were more complicated. "The fire marshal's report says there's an 80% chance it was lightning."

"I *know* it was lightning," Gabe says, "but what I want to know, is *why*."

"You tell me how you dodged a bullet or, was it, maybe, you took one deliberately, and I'll help you figure why Ascension didn't fare as well."

"You think I know who fired at me?" Gabe asks.

"You seem to think I'd know why Mother Nature would fire at a church," Peter says.

"You ain't involved in no turf war."

"Wanna bet?" Peter stops to consider. "The human heart. That's our turf. Does your hiding in our basement have something to do with that?"

"What d'ya mean?"

"I almost never help strangers, especially young ones. You should know. It can be dangerous, especially if you suspect they don't need help. But something, or someone, told me you are looking for a friend. I'm probably not the best one you could imagine. But, I'm here. At least I can remind you of what you are looking for. Am I making any sense?"

"Would you like some more chicken?" Gabriel gathers in the empty boxes, napkins and bones.

Peter is surprised. "Yeah, sure."

"I'll pay," Gabe says. He looks back at Peter over his shoulder as he heads inside. "More coleslaw, or would you rather have potato salad?"

"Whatever you're having."

Before the afternoon is out, Peter White knows about Gabriel Luna's desperate plan to extricate himself and a young friend from Avenida Menudo, their street gang.

"It's the drugs. I don't want to be bringing kids to that. Drugs is a death certificate. And doin' 'em can give you AIDS."

Gabe waited months for the drop truck to show up with a new driver at the wheel. "Last night, boom. It finally happened. As soon as he asked me, I told him 'no, I ain't Luna. I seen Luna. He was here just awhile ago, but he left.'"

The truck sped away without leaving any drugs and, key to Gabe's plan, without taking the cash he was ponying. Sonny Mendoza, the other horse in the delivery duo, was waiting for Gabe at their rendezvous. "Like we planned, Sonny got out the tool we'd stashed a while back, and he shot me." Gabe took one on the arm at fairly close range. Sonny kept the money while Gabe proceeded to the clubhouse to report he'd been robbed while waiting for the drop.

"I can tell a good story when I have to."

The wound, and the forthrightness, had offered proof. With the money, Sonny and Gabe planned to go to Mexico, to live with Gabe's grandparents for awhile or even, an uncle. The hitch was not clearing the idea with Sonny's mother.

"Even though she's got a dozen kids and never time for him, Mrs. Mendoza said she would spill everything. She didn't want Sonny leavin' in the middle of the night. She was drunk some, too, I think. And real sarcastic when she caught him. He'd had all the advantages. Why did he think the family had gone to the trouble of coming here in the first place? So he could go *back?* Why would he do that, when he had all the advantages?"

Sonny's mother didn't want to hear that her son's troubles are life-threatening. He can leave the gang whenever he wants to, she says. She refuses to hear what he is up against on the streets. When he came in for a suitcase, she forced him to explain. Then she locked Sonny in a closet and took a butcher knife after Gabe. That's when he ran to Ascension. "Maybe four in the morning. I was really scared."

This is the way Bliss got the story from her warden before her appearance in family court on Gabriel Luna's behalf six months later.

9

Life After Stained Glass

''Bliss has this thing about her independence," Sam says to Andrea Marvin. "She's overlooked my needs at times when I could have used her support. So I don't suppose she's looking for any support from me just now."

"Hold on." Andrea lifts a hand. "You glossed over an important thought when you said Bliss hasn't given you the support you needed. What's that about?"

"Sally. And James. Our children. I've put off probing those losses. Not just with you. With myself."

"And with God?" Andrea asks.

"You *would* twig to that. Damn, does nothing get by you?"

"Haven't you had to counsel people whose infants have died?"

"Well, I only lost *one* child to death," Sam says. "She was perfect. And I'm sure Sally sings with the angels. Much as I would have loved to watch her grow, I never feel that far from her. I think of her as living in stained glass. You know, facing both ways. It's my son I'm concerned about." Sam chokes. Tears stream down his face as he continues. "Bliss simply gave him away. Just like that, she let James go out of our life."

Andrea remains silent although she feels stunned. Finally, she asks, "Would you like to explain that?"

"I want an explanation myself. I deserve one! We took this woman into our home to look after our newly adopted son. Bliss somehow became convinced that Sharon, the babysitter, was our boy's natural mother. I don't think she had any hard evidence. At any rate, just before we moved back here to California, the babysitter disappeared. She left us a note saying she was taking James to New Mexico, to be reunited with his biological father. They'd decided to become a family, the note said. Bliss didn't protest, didn't even appear to grieve. If anything, I'd say she seemed relieved. She lobbied very hard against involving the police, which I very nearly did anyway. She kept saying the natural mother has a right to change her mind about an adoption. But it had been nearly three years. I tried to tell her they have to change their minds during the first year. All Bliss did was insist that Sharon *had* changed her mind during the first year—which was why she'd taken the job with us."

"And this left you . . ." Andrea trails off.

"Feeling helpless and impotent."

"And?" Andrea prompts.

"And?" Sam answers. Then he jokes, "Read my mind, please." His therapist always insists she won't do that.

"Angry!" Andrea shouts lifting both fists and shaking them close to her ears.

Sam looks as though a gust of wind has caught him in the face. "I suppose so, yes."

"You suppose so! Do you plan to sit in this shit 'til only a holy man from India would venture near you? Do you understand me?" she shouts. "This is how I sound when I'm just a little bit angry." Andrea drops her volume slightly. "Do you want to work on this crap or not?"

"I don't know how."

"We start by looking at it, and looking at you sitting in it. What kind of a wimp lets his wife give away his only son? Why does he do that? Come on. Right now. Enlighten me on this one, Sam."

"He doesn't know any better?"

"Quite the contrary," Andrea argues. "I think he does."

"He doesn't have enough self esteem to stand up to the woman he loves?"

"Keep going," Andrea prompts. "Dig down. This is your cheerleader talking." She waves a closed fist again.

Sam begins slowly still speaking of himself in the third person. "He doesn't believe the woman he loves has as much strength as he thought she had. She isn't really a bombshell. She's fragile. An eggshell maybe."

"And because she's pretended to strengths she doesn't have, she's let him down," Andrea suggests.

"She's let him down once too often." Sam puts his head in his hand. It doesn't feel right to blame Bliss. It hurts him.

"How does that feel, being let down once too often?"

"Shitty."

"You bet it does. At least we have got you feeling. Feeling your feelings. I'm afraid that cleaning it up is something we are going to have to tackle next time." Andrea taps her watch. It's her traditional two-minute warning.

"I've felt it before. It's just that I feel guilty dragging anyone down to my level," Sam says quietly.

"Since you pay me to find your level, Sam, you can drop the guilt trip here. Get on with the task of equipping yourself to shovel shit." Andrea slaps her hands on her knees and stands up.

As Sam stands, he turns and mimes flushing an imaginary toilet. "And here I thought shit could be flushed. Whoosh. All gone."

"Don't ride a metaphor too far. Like some wives, words pretend to strengths they don't have," Andrea says. "If it worked that way," she gestures toward his imaginary toilet, "we psychologists would be burned at the stake for treating clients one at a time when any ritual mumbo jumble for the masses, maybe even at the Masses, would do." Andrea opens the office door.

"You do that deliberately, don't you?" Sam says.

"What?"

"Leave me with something to think about on my drive home."

"Why, Sam, I thought you'd know by now. I do *everything* deliberately." She reaches to him for their traditional closing hug.

* * *

THORNDIKE, SHRIVER & ARMACOST
Attorneys at Law
Los Angeles, California

August 10, 1990

Dear Bliss,

I am more than happy to supply the information your vestry has requested without charge. I appreciate the offer of a retainer, but my dear mother would roll over in her grave if I were to accept money from her favorite parish. My memories of attending Ascension as a child are happy ones, and I'm saddened that your congregation is presented with troubles of this magnitude.

As to the position of the national church in a situation like this, I see three relevant section in our canons:

1. All buildings and property connected with the Episcopal Church (and their contents) are to be kept adequately insured. (TITLE 1.6.1)

We know Church of the Ascension is covered by the Church Insurance Corporation (CIC). What we don't know is whether their first settlement offer will be the one your vestry should accept. Most churches that wait for a second appraisal receive a better settlement. This slows down your ability to undertake immediate planning, but as I understand it, you face slowdowns with the Diocese anyway because your coverage may be seen to include them as a co-insured.

For all intents and purposes, legally, Ascension is no longer the group that continues to meet at the site on Sunday mornings and conduct business from a temporary storefront office, but rather, it is that insurance check, still forthcoming from CIC. I know this seems impersonal. But legally, the Diocese has what is known as a "contingent interest" or an interest in the "contingent remainder" of your church. If you were to disappear into the woodwork, by joining other churches (corporately or individually), and didn't use the insurance money to rebuild, the Diocese would claim the proceeds and the property itself.

2. Section 4 of the above Title 1 reads:

All real and personal property held by a congregation is held in trust for this Church and Diocese. This in no way limits the authority of a congregation over its property so long as it remains subject to this Church, its Constitutions and Canons.

I share your alarm. Should the chancellor downgrade Ascension to mission status, the implication is that your congregation would be subject to direct diocesan oversight.

3. The national church requires a parish, congregation or mission to obtain the written consent of the Bishop and Standing Committee prior to taking on any financial encumbrance of its property (by way of a lien or mortgage).

This means that if you can't rebuild for the settlement monies offered, or if, as you fear, the bishop isn't interested in seeing you rebuild, you might find yourselves unable to complete a building project without first raising all the needed funds since your endowment precludes its use for capital improvements. I'll offer you additional advice after your September meeting with Bishop Sprockett. My best to you, Bliss, and to your people. I'm sure you'll be granted the wisdom to see this whole thing through.

Yours very truly,
Ernest Shriver

10

Where Were You When Elvis Died?

Friday, September 7, 1990

*B*liss agreed to visit psychologist Andrea Marvin for a joint session with Sam this afternoon. By coincidence, the appointment falls on the twenty-second anniversary of Sally's crib death.

"How are you feeling?" Andrea addresses her opening question to both clients.

Bliss begins. "I'm feeling defensive. Sam has a year up on me with you. I don't think I can catch up with him."

"Catch up with me?" Sam sounds surprised.

Andrea merely nods in assent to the interchange.

"I've noticed a loosening up in you, Sam. You're comfortable talking about things," Bliss says. "I feel as if I'm here to match your progress somehow. It . . ." she trails off.

"Did you come just because Sam asked you to?" Andrea asks.

"I feel a need to defend myself. You know, they tell SIDS parents they aren't to blame for their baby's death, but the instant you put it behind you, everyone acts as if you are cold and unfeeling."

"Did you mourn the loss of your daughter?" Andrea asks.

Bliss turns to Sam. He says, "I think we did grieve Sally's death. Yes. In fact, that was the only other time we saw a counselor together."

"Sally was almost too perfect," Bliss says. "It was strange. As if she was so spiritual she didn't have the heart to carve out an ego for herself. She seemed to be somewhere else most of the time. Not like other babies who coo and cry. When she was no longer with us, I felt as though *she'd* chosen to return to the Light. That sounds mystical. I guess it is. Just thinking of Sally, I'm held by a powerful, but delicate Silence."

"That's how it is for me," Sam adds. "Sally is a free spirit. She can look in any direction. She was born fourteen months after we were married, and she died before she'd lived out her fourteenth month. Most SIDS victims succumb younger, we were told. The number fourteen has seemed perfect and magical to me ever since. Like Pike's introducing me to the fourteen calendar patterns." Sam glances at the clock on the wall. It's precisely fourteen minutes after four. The women follow his eyes and note the minuscule coincidence.

"Did you also mourn the loss of your son?" Andrea asks her clients. Sam looks to Bliss and purses his lips. He raises his eyebrows as if to confess that he's already said too much on this subject to Andrea.

Bliss's tone is almost accusatory. "So *that's* what this is about." She brings the heels of her hands together, rolls the palms inward slowly and folds her fingers down. Andrea notices that Bliss's left thumb sits naturally atop the right, the opposite of how Sam clasps his hands. She applauds herself for picking up the detail. Something in the literature will remind her of the cerebral significance of that unconscious choice. It escapes her at the moment.

"You sound as if you think Sam and I conspired to rope you into this session," Andrea suggests.

Bliss sits silently. The other two wait.

"James did not *die*," Bliss begins at last. "Our son, if we must persist in thinking of James that way, was taken out of our lives by his natural parents."

"He was kidnapped by our babysitter," Sam says firmly.

"The babysitter was his own mother," Bliss adds with equal doggedness.

"She was in our employ." Sam lets his voice rise. "She was not mothering him those two years we paid her for her services. She was *tending* him on *our* behalf. We were his legal parents."

"James is fourteen now," Bliss says, trying to detach herself from the past. To Sam, the observation comes like a tracer bullet exploding in his ears. *Fourteen.*

"Not a day goes by," Bliss continues, "that I don't offer prayers for James. But, I don't feel sorry for him. I don't feel sorry for myself or for his parents. What is it? Am I supposed to feel sorry for you, Sam?"

"We made a mistake," he says. "We should have reported it

to the police. He went missing. We should have searched for him, retrieved him and raised him ourselves. Then, at least, we would know what's become of him."

"Did you feel this way at the time?" Bliss asks.

"I don't remember. You were insistent; that's about all I recall about the time."

"I was insistent because I had known from the first day she came to work for us that Sharon wanted her son back. I hoped in the beginning that she would change her mind." Bliss directs her comments quite pointedly to Andrea now. "But when it became possible for Sharon to reunite with James' father, she left us and she took her son with her. We were in the middle of making plans to move back to California. Sam had gone through a bout with depression. It's harder than you might think to land two clergy appointments within driving distance of each other. How could we hunt Sharon down like a criminal? She'd let me know her intentions from the very beginning. I tried to protect everyone. It was a very difficult time."

"So the reason you held off bonding with James," Sam asks, "was because you thought Sharon wanted him back?"

Bliss stands. She makes eye contact with Andrea to check that it's all right for her to walk about as she talks. "I seem to think better on my feet," she says. Andrea's shrug is a go-ahead. "I wasn't aware that you felt I hadn't bonded with James. But it would be true to say I didn't really mother him. Sharon's wishes probably had something to do with that." Bliss fingers the spines of several books on the bookshelf and walks toward the corner where a fluffy green and yellow parakeet is caged. "At the time she came to us, in September of 1976, Sharon was well within her legal time limit to reclaim the baby. She showed me the paperwork. She was ready to submit it. I may have made a mistake in persuading her to stay with us and act as his nanny."

"Why didn't you tell me she wanted him?" Sam says.

"You were just, so . . ." Bliss searches for a word. "So fragile on the subject of children, Sam. We'd tried to have another," Bliss says, crossing back toward Andrea. "And I thought if Sharon had given him up once, chances were she'd change her mind again once she saw the kind of family we were. Of course, she didn't have a legal leg to stand on when she took him in June of '78. She'd never filed those papers with the court. I was the one who knew of her change of heart, who knew I had kept her from filing. She'd confided in me and I had acted in my own best interest in keeping her from putting her change of heart on the record." Bliss sighs and resumes her seat. "Sam, do you remember the night we learned that Elvis had died?"

"Your folks had come to our place for a barbecue to celebrate."

"It was James's first birthday," Bliss tells Andrea.

"God, I haven't thought of this in so long," Sam says. "Donald had gotten James a red wagon and we laughed because it was so ahead of time. More like a piece of furniture we'd have to use than a toy for the baby."

"And we cried. Elvis was dead. Sharon asked if she could be excused, and went to her room. When I went to the bathroom, I could hear her weeping. She was sobbing as if she'd lost a member of the family."

"I remember that she played Elvis records continuously for days after," Sam says.

"It was about then, that fall, sometime after my father's retirement, that I told you that Sharon was James's biological mother, and that she had wanted him back. Admittedly, my motives were not the best in deciding not to track her down when she left. I have the impression James's father graduated from high school that year. We'd helped Sharon get her equivalency that spring by correspondence."

"What were your motives, if not the best?" Andrea asks.

"Selfish. I'd convinced myself I wasn't the best mother for James. Sam is probably right. I *hadn't* bonded with him. When Sharon said she was leaving to marry James' father, I was frightened. She loved James in a way that moved me. How could I raise him without her? Sam, you matched her affection and I never fully appreciated that."

"Are you saying you *knew* she was leaving with James?" Sam asks.

"No. I didn't know. But I feel certain Sharon knew I wouldn't be able to pursue her. Not after what we'd shared. We communicated, how can I say this, subliminally. What had happened, was that she became more like a daughter to me than James did a son." Hearing the impact of her own statement shakes Bliss. She reaches for a tissue from the well-placed Scotties box. "I haven't said this. I nurtured Sharon. I didn't really nurture the baby, *her* baby. And when they were gone, it was Sharon I missed the most."

Andrea waits. Neither client is falling apart, although both are in tears. "It surprises me," she says, "that you and Sam can sit here and have this conversation so rationally. You haven't gotten into fights about it? Bliss, I hear a longing in your voice—as if you've waited for years to be questioned about this. Do you and Sam generally leave things unsaid?"

"Just gut-wrenching things, wouldn't you say?"

Sam doesn't answer. So Bliss goes on, addressing Andrea. "Sam doesn't tell me what goes into the morning journals he locks away, and I don't complain about the hell I go through to have the same career he's been handed on a silver platter. He can see all the sexism without my sniveling about it."

"You know about Sam's diaries?"

"I know *of* them. Like Sam knew *of* my behavior with Sharon. Like he knows *of* the fire at Ascension."

"Are there things you'd like him to know that he doesn't?" Andrea asks.

"There are certainly things causing me grief, more grief than I'd ever imagined I'd have to face in such a tiny parish. But I don't whimper as a rule."

"Do you want a shoulder to cry on?" Andrea prods.

"Why?"

"Moral support. To let your husband know what's happening with you, for a change. You said you noticed *he* was warming up. Perhaps *you* could do with some of that?"

"Am I cold? Damn. That's the last thing I want to be. That's what I always hated in my father." Bliss eyes the parakeet in the corner of the room. *What is perching in the recesses of my mind?* Bliss thinks. "May I have a glass of water?"

"With or without ice?" Andrea asks. She opens the door of an apartment-sized refrigerator beside the door to the outer office.

"Ice, please."

Sam gets out of his chair and joins his wife on the love seat. Putting an arm around her, he whispers, "Determined to reinforce those fatherly qualities?" Bliss elbows him, but leans into his warmth. Before taking the water, she reaches up and strokes her husband's moist cheeks.

"I never wanted to make you cry," she says, "but I guess that's something we both need to learn to do."

"Tears can be," Sam pauses, "as good as sex, I think."
Andrea hands Bliss the glass of water. "Cry me a river."

* * *

At his private session ten days later, Sam asks Andrea to look at his journal entry concerning those born on a Monday in a number Three year. According to Pike, those are the years in which members of the Tribe of Judah are born.

After receiving the names of "arrivals"—Cher, Barry Manilow, Betty Ford, Melvin Belli, Sam Gallup, Chancellor Helmut Schmidt and Geraldine Ferraro—Sam had written, "I don't want to listen for departures."

"Fine," his mentor had answered. "Some listeners require more coincidental evidence than others. We aren't able to 'guarantee' departures, anyway. No problem. We'll keep our best guesses to ourselves. A lifetime is an arbitrary learning device at best."

Sam had asked about astrology. And Pike had answered, "Astrology is a hierarchical science. In the coming age, people will require that the spheres influencing life be seen within the human body itself. They'll demand a system in which every disciplined devotee achieves mastery. Creative astrologers will incorporate individual energy profiles with astrological information. You'll hear talk of Monday-born Gemini's, Tuesday-born Gemini's and the like."

When Sam had inquired as to why he was considered an appropriate transcriber of the complex Calendar of Chariots information, he'd been told, "The best channels are those who are either profoundly religious or profoundly atheist. Being fearless in the face of being emptied, and lacking anticipation when being filled, are the qualities you bring to this inter-dimensional endeavor. Your predisposition to things scientific opens the door even wider."

Andrea looks up. "If you're ready to share this material, why don't you bring some of it to our next session with Bliss?"

"Hmm."

"Just hmm? Not okay?"

"Maybe it's no coincidence my diaries date from Sally's death and gain momentum with Pike's departure."

"And?"

"I vacillate between thinking of my journals as personal or as destined for public consumption. Here, I realize that I vacillate between seeing the private and public aspects of people in my life. It feels as if I've been born to eliminate the boundaries between have and have not, but I'm struggling with that. It's like I don't have all the information—the technical, scientific type information—that I need."

"How important is that?"

"Is what?"

"Having all the information," Andrea says. "It seems to me Pike overloads you with information. Even an atheist could take dictation from him, he says."

Sam likes to harass Andrea in harmless ways about her professed atheism. Bringing up that word has become a hallmark of theirs. If Andrea were to approach him for Christian instruction the way he has come to her for psychological advice, he likes to think he would be up to it. But she would see inside the patterns of faith-building in ways other people don't. It is hard to imagine being her spiritual mentor.

"An atheist willing to go to heaven, I should think."

"I don't need heaven," Andrea volunteers. "If it's there, I'll deal with it then. Can't be bothered now."

Sam brightens. "You haven't volunteered that much spiritual information about yourself before."

"'I can't be bothered' is *spiritual* information?"

"Via negativa. You, in essence, challenge God to let you witness creation at your own pace. Heaven, if it is there, will come in due time. Doubting is a survival skill. God-given, I would say. You wouldn't. And you may be right. Humankind *could* be fantasizing everything that isn't spirit. Or, as they say in the jargon, 'we are creating our own reality.'"

"Do you preach this way ordinarily?"

"There's only one way to find out how I preach ordinarily. But a year ago, you made me promise not to convert you." Sam lifts his right hand as if swearing in a court of law. "I consider myself under oath not to preach to you."

"I did ask for that, didn't I? I didn't suppose your faith would sneak up on me, that's for sure."

Andrea considers for a moment what *is* sneaking up on her—the animal magnetism of this cloth-bound clergyman whose head is a tangle of salt and pepper curls that find their own style. He's fit for Mount Olympus. Even with the collar. He seldom comes in street clothes. The collar is part of the package. "The cross I must bear," he said once, explaining that in public priests aren't treated with deference anymore. Outright contempt or suspicion are common. She wonders if ten more years will turn his curls completely white. How dashing snowy snarls would be against his perfectly tanned face. Looking, you realize Sam's always been handsome. And this reticence he has to showing himself turns his everyday good looks into an all-out turn-on. His irreverent body is more dangerous, at close quarters, than any religious notions it fosters.

* * *

OFFICE OF THE URBAN DEACON
Diocese of Los Angeles

September 20, 1990

Dear Reverend Birch,
    Let me summarize what I discussed with your vestry ten days ago. I suggested that you need to establish *a place of temporary worship. The alternatives appear to be:*
    1) accept the invitation of the hospital chaplain to use the chapel there,
    2) approach a local funeral parlor
    3) attend Epiphany (combining with them at their usual gathering time) or, of course,
    4) continue crowding into the present "charcoal chapel."
    I'm concerned that proper demolition has been delayed. I agreed to speak with the diocesan treasurer concerning an advance (on insurance proceeds) to facilitate cleanup.
    When we got down to the meat of the reason I'd come, to present Bishop Sprockett's alternatives to rebuilding Ascension where it is, I found tremendous opposition to the very suggestion that Ascension consider relocating. Even if you stay where you are, the congregation must undertake a needs assessment. (You indicated by phone this week that records of an assessment you'd only recently completed were destroyed in the fire. My ignorance of that may, indeed, have sparked the frustrated responses I didn't fully appreciate.)
    I learned you had gotten word that you can expect a

settlement of $698,714. But your vestry feels it should hold out for more. I proceeded to indicate what $700,000 buys in today's market. I raised questions regarding the pledging base you might draw upon during a building-fund campaign.

And, of course, I asked the most unpopular question, "Is it good stewardship for a group so small to rebuild?" Some seemed to think that by asking the question I was implying an answer. I don't mean to do that; the question is yours to pray about. Bliss, you indicated you don't have the skills to supervise a construction site. And no one among Ascension's officers indicated they'd be able to do that either.

I realize everyone was disappointed Bishop Sprockett could not attend. Complications arise in his scheduling. But I feel we made a productive beginning and this letter will serve to update him as to your present situation.

Sincerely,
Elizabeth Sparks, Urban Deacon

11

Forbidden Fruit: A Full Disclosure

Monday, September 24, 1990

"If I watch," Andrea Marvin says at the beginning of Sam's session, "could you write in your spiritual diary? You know, receive Pike's dictation? Here. In this room. In that chair?"

Sam beams like a youngster auditioning for the school play. "I could try. Why would we do that?"

"To look at the finished product. Would you let me read it?"

"I suppose. But it might take ten minutes to get a page."

Andrea hands Sam an empty spiral-bound notebook. He fishes for a pen from the inside breast pocket of his linen sports jacket, then looks around the room as if putting drop cloths over the furniture. Opening the notebook, he draws a line down the middle of the page, putting "them" above the left column and "me" above the right. Very shortly, he begins writing:

THEM	ME
Why are you willing to do this for the good doctor?	*Proof of sanity.*
Your sanity has never been in question, Samuel, only the quality and potential of your mediumship. You are, how shall we put this, a reluctant medium.	*Mediumship is not mainstream behavior.*
Let's test your ability by involving the curious doctor.	

We have a gentle spirit coming forward who says his name was Joseph. He would like to send greetings to his Andrea, whom he loves very much. He says he once received a lock of her hair in the mail. That piece of her baby fine hair is still nestled in the envelope in which he received it. Andrea will find it near the bottom of a box of her family's papers in the attic of her mother's home. As she searches for this love letter from Maria to Joe Marvin, she'll be reminded of a father's caring—a perpetual, continuing love. Proof of that is seen in this, as Joe reaches to her through you from an "other" dimension.

Will I ever feel stupid if you're wrong?

You don't have to persuade her of anything. Certainty is a gift. Or, like interest drawn on monies left in the bank. It translates into the divine message: "I Am is always with you."

Will Andrea's father watch over her as she looks for this lock of hair? Will he "be there" should she happen to find it?

She will have to experience the search and provide an answer to that (if she chooses to).

Sam looks up from the notebook. Andrea is still in her armchair on the other side of the gray coffee table. She opens her eyes and smiles.

"I decided to meditate while you worked. I thought you might have more trouble getting started," she says.

"No. It's like tuning in a radio station. It doesn't take long if you've done it before."

"Was anything different about tuning in here?"

"Definitely. The content is totally pointed to the occasion." He hands Andrea the notebook.

"Do you know what this says?" she asks without looking up.

"Yes."

"You weren't in any kind of trance when you wrote it?"

Andrea doesn't make her comment a question, but Sam hears it that way. He shakes his head, no.

"Where does it come from? I don't mean alpha, theta or delta state. That we could measure mechanically. I mean, where does it feel like it's coming from?"

"Well," Sam says, "I pull it in from between my ears the way a magician lifts a dove from the palm of his hand. It's not clear like a voice, but an impression that I'm able to put into words. These particular impressions," he gestures to the spiral notebook, "a lock of hair, a man's name . . . and names are generally very difficult to get clear on, are very specific. Go ahead, have a look."

Andrea reads the dialogue quickly.

"So?" Sam is anxious to know her response.

"I'm shocked actually. I have pooh-poohed the idea of contact with the dead. A parlor game, I would have said, where impeccable research is played for the amazement of onlookers. When you are dead, you are dead and gone. So I thought. Mediumship, a cruel hoax. But I sat here. No tricks. And this *has* significance for me. You weren't trying to impress me. You didn't even know I was going to ask you to try this. But, what you've written matches what's happening in my life."

"Really." It's Sam's turn to feel surprise. Then he turns the tables. "Does it inspire confidence?"

Andrea wiggles a finger at him. "I understand this better now. Being singled out for revelation is more of a challenge than an honor."

"Would you like me to do some more listening for you?"

"No." She lifts one hand to her ear and one to her mouth the way the DJ on *Laugh-In* used to do. "I believe I'll be able to find my station. At least, I can recognize the music."

"You're hearing? Just like that?"

"A door opened as I meditated. I saw my father, like in a dream. You know, I've almost reached the box your angels mention. I'm digging through things my mother had for fifty, sixty years. My dad, Joe Marvin, was serving in Korea when I was born. It would have been just like mom to have clipped a curl to send to him. He would have cherished her letters. My family believes in mementos. I've learned a lot about my parents this last month looking at the things they saved."

"Are they dead?" Sam asks cautiously.

"Only my dad. So, how does this sit?"

"I'm relieved," Sam says. "I would have felt the fool if there was no confirmation available."

"And how *do* you feel?" Andrea presses.

"I feel—heady. You asked for this. It would be nice if . . ." Andrea feels like she can finish this sentence, but she waits for Sam to do it. ". . . if Bliss could. . ." But Sam can't get himself to the end of that thought.

"Would you like to share some of your Pike material with her? Next joint session? Are you ready?"

"I need to think about that."

"Why?"

"Because she hasn't asked."

"Fair enough. But locking your journaling away not only protects your privacy, it prevents your becoming the intuitive you could be if you opened up."

"Andrea, I don't know *how*."

"In my profession, a gift like yours is coveted. When a person can filter *any* profound process for individuals, he is in demand. I think I was prompted to push for a live demonstration. Confirming your skills was my intention, but it seems as if getting my attention was precisely what your angels, your guides, Pike . . ." Andrea interrupts herself. "How do you address them?"

"They have called themselves The Seventy. I don't usually try to sort out who's who. Sometimes it feels as if we are several, gathered around a table in a conference room. Other times, it seems as if I am on the phone with just one party. I can always feel his energy when Pike is present. And I sense his love in the group even when I don't 'hear' his voice. Since I don't talk about them, I haven't had to worry about what to call them."

"When you say energy . . ." Andrea doesn't finish because a rush comes upon her that answers the question she was trying to ask. It tells her more about her attraction to Sam Garland than she was prepared to hear. "Oh, my."

Sam observes. "I guess they do want your attention."

Andrea lifts a hand as if to protect her face. "Forgive me. I seem to be turning the focus onto myself."

"Are you blushing?"

Andrea buries her head in both palms.

Sam feels his own cheeks flush. "*Jim?*" It's as if this patently sexual energy both he and Andrea are experiencing might be explained best by the deceased clergyman who handpicked Sam's bride.

"I'm sorry," Andrea says, "this is so unprofessional of me." She stands and moves toward the door. "It would probably be best if we just end this early."

Sam pushes himself back into his chair more deeply. He knows what he wants to say, but he needs a deep breath in order to say it. "It's been years, Andrea, since . . . well, since I had to edge my way around a woman who . . . was feeling what I imagine you are."

"Years?"

"It used to happen all the time. When I worked for Pike, I had to make a put-off speech probably once a week. 'I'm flattered but . . .' Now, people see Bliss and I don't have to explain. Flirting with a clergyman is a little more difficult, I suppose, when you would be tempting him to be unfaithful to another member of the cloth."

"Bliss's being beautiful has more to do with it than her collar."

"Can you believe? I take her looks for granted. It's hard to keep on seeing the marvelous as marvelous when you live with it."

"Sam, please get up. We need to put this session behind us, not draw it out."

"Right." Sam stands. His body is more than a little aware of itself. It's a happy sensation just this side of a thrill. He can feel where his clothes are touching his skin, where his belt is shifting at his waist. After Andrea closes the door behind him—without offering the usual goodbye hug—Sam just stands with his back against it, looking in the direction of the receptionist until she looks his way. He signals, then, as though he has forgotten something, turns and opens the door himself. Andrea is fanning her face with a file folder. She lays a palm over her throat and looks inquisitively at Sam. He smiles, bows just slightly, and says, as if to confirm something, "*Everything* is deliberate with you, right?"

"Sit down," Andrea says firmly. Sam closes the door and returns to his chair. Andrea returns to hers and for a full minute, the two of them look at one another without speaking.

Sam can feel his demons breaking loose—his fear that his fantasies are circumspect, that he'll never be as free as he was in his youth; his fear of making a spectacle of himself, of being found in a compromising situation and of having to tell Bliss he's been unfaithful. Like now. Andrea as Salome. If she were to dance toward him, could he resist? *You've waited so long for someone else to release you,* his devil says.

Emotion fills Andrea as well. She has tapped into Sam's soul where the energy is simultaneously painful and pleasant.

"There's so much at stake," Sam finally says.

"I'm strong enough to share my dreams or to keep them out of this," Andrea begins, "because making Andrea Marvin's dreams come true is not what our association is intended to be about."

"But you can feel it, can't you? The ground is shifting."

"It's dizzying," Andrea confesses.

"I'm thinking about you," Sam says deliberately, "in a way that makes me feel as if I've *already* committed adultery. Does thinking make it so? God, if only it did. I'd give the world to be able to act on these thoughts."

Andrea brushes a tear from the corner of her eye. "Maybe saying it is enough."

"Don't we wish." Sam sounds almost tired as he stands and moves to the love seat. "If we don't consummate this . . ." Andrea pushes herself up out of her chair. "Thank you," Sam says. He combs the fingers of his right hand through his hair, first at the right temple. Then, the left.

Andrea comes half way and then sits on the floor.

"I already had you *here*," Sam protests, patting the space beside himself. He blows Andrea a kiss.

"I would never want it said that I seduced you." Andrea

sounds forlorn. Why does the happiness of forty years have to be crammed into these stolen moments? She whispers so softly Sam doesn't hear, "It would be better not to know."

"We've come this far," Sam says.

"We don't have to take this any further."

"I'll take the blame." Sam pulls the rigid plastic support out of his clerical collar and gets up. In one fluid motion he walks to where Andrea is sitting. But he doesn't sit. He reaches for her hand to help her up. "There's something we've never spoken of," he says.

"I think we have," she answers. She pulls Sam down beside her. He doesn't resist her kisses. So much is routine in his ordered life. But these kisses ring through him with the perfect spontaneity of a sabbatical. Sam's soul takes wing. The glorious seconds of discovery unfold as if they were days. A honeymoon. Sam flies to his own Garden of Eden where exploration gives way to all that is more insistent. He debates with the doorkeeper of Paradise as Andrea takes charge, "*How can this be forbidden fruit. If forbidden, it would be impossible.*"

* * *

Driving home, Sam thinks of the half-dozen clergy he knows who keep girlfriends on the side, women they supposedly sleep with regularly. One cathedral dean flies his mistress in for all the national conferences he attends. She's such a fixture at these sessions other priests question him as to her whereabouts if she misses a gathering.

Sam thinks again. Which dean is that? Who told him the story? Is it an urban legend he's allowed himself to file as truth? Why has he been willing to believe it all these years? Why is a concubine fodder for the macho mill? Sam Garland has never been sympathetic to promiscuity. But still, it exists. He could forgive Philip Dick his revelations about the fictional Timothy Archer, for he'd been taken aback more than once by the level of tolerance certain people displayed in the face of a bishop's open philandering. It was the notoriety that had been embarrassing.

Tonight, as Sam entertains the possibility of incorporating a mistress into his own pattern, he knows the ambivalence of men who fear being reported through channels. *What a comedown*, Sam lectures himself. *My midlife crisis is sexual, just like everyone else's.*

How foolish to suppose it had anything to do with angels on my back. But courting the idea of Andrea, Sam finds, makes him think of nothing so much as the prospect of bedding his Bliss. *Will she be suspicious if my ardor is in high gear on a Monday? How absurd.* In his search for the truth concerning his wife's perceptions, Sam's discernment fails him. There's a ball of confusion in his belly wound tighter than the mammoth collection of string he kept at the foot of his bed as a youngster, to which he added a little each day.

What explanation does a husband owe a wife when he surveys the limits of fidelity? It's a question Sam has faced on several occasions, but never with himself as the proposed infidel. He's told others that the confession that is good for the soul should not be used to heap grief upon another. Now he can appreciate the symptomatic relief that advice gives. Insidiously, he finds his imagination running back to Andrea. She's the one who's opened him to these fantasies. *Carry on a tryst with someone whose confidence you already have. A silent partner needs a silent partner.*

Now, fingering the button on his automatic garage door opener, Sam grieves having left Andrea so abruptly. *I left her to fend for herself. What a bastard I am. Back to square one: guilty.*

"Having left undone those things I ought to have done," Sam says aloud, shutting off the engine. The comment is directed nowhere in particular. A priest can't confess his failure to consummate an illicit encounter to the Powers That Be. Sam rubs the inside of his thighs before shifting his weight. *Manhood. It threatens everything and promises what?* Fragrances from years past seem to waft into the car, tangibly sweet. "If only I'd asked your name, sweet one," Sam whispers to a long ago beach bitch. *You were, indeed, my first love.*

12

Hannah Thomas, Where Are You?

CHURCH OF THE ASCENSION
Spreading the Gospel since 1863

October 2, 1990

Dear Bishop Sprockett,
    The vestry of Church of the Ascension respectfully requests that you meet with us soon. We need to hear your thoughts concerning our future.
    With all due respect, the Urban Deacon's recent presentation was disturbing. Two people left the meeting in disgust. Ms. Spark's idea of building a daycare facility is not without merit. We will consider it. But her agenda does not rise from our ashes. We need the ear of a pastor who can sense where we are. And presently, we aren't on track for achieving a good working relationship with Deacon Sparks. So we ask to meet with you, face to face.
    We continue to hold services on site despite our inability to get a speedy financial settlement. We don't expect to mortgage our land or to sell it. Such decisions would have to be cleared with you in any event. We want to involve you in planning the restoration of our structure. Some folks want things just as they were; others hope to take this opportunity to make changes. Our priest is understanding, and we rely on her leadership.
    May we suggest four possible meeting dates: November 6 or 7, November 29 or 30. If these aren't acceptable, please suggest times more suitable. Thank you. Your personal involvement is necessary, I feel, to bring this matter to a successful outcome.
    Sincerely,
    Peter White, Warden

* * *

At the time he would ordinarily be writing in his morning journal, Sam Garland, the Reverend Sam Garland, is driving in a disreputable district of Los Angeles, where he is hoping to find some ladies of the evening still plying their trade.

In San Francisco, in the summer of '52, when Sam first wanted a hooker, he had no car, and no courage to approach a working girl without one. He was just seventeen and the lady he wanted to spend time with was probably pushing forty. That didn't matter. She attracted him. She distracted him. And, to Sam's dismay, she never even noticed him hanging around. He was as good as invisible. They never spoke. Now, it's tragic to him that he never learned her name. More upsetting than his never having gone to bed with her.

The young woman who agrees to climb in—after seeing three ten dollar bills on the passenger seat—doesn't wish to talk as they pull away. Finally, she asks, "What d'ya want?"

Sam doesn't answer.

"French, Greek, Geek, Missionary?"

"I'd like to talk," Sam answers.

"Shit. You ain't no john. Lemme out. Lemme out, mister. I made a mistake. Here, shit. Here's your money."

Sam is incredulous. "You're not afraid of me?" His isn't wearing his collar. But a turtleneck tee makes him feel as if he's in his usual garb. Sam isn't used to anyone's being afraid of him.

"Cops just love to talk."

"I'm harmless. I swear I won't turn you in. Can't we just spend some time? If I told you who I am, you'd laugh," Sam says.

"Why? You one of them no good preachers?" she fairly chortles.

Sam involuntarily copies her laugh. "I'm quite a good one actually. And I have never picked up a hooker before. Ask the Man Upstairs if you don't believe me." Sam is upset with himself. He had no intention of revealing so much.

"Sure." The lady smiles broadly. "They all like to pretend it's the first time. Shit. What is it, then? The little woman doesn't understand you? Trouble at home?"

"Trouble away from home," Sam says. "Someone *does* understand me."

"You're tryin' to forget."

"Maybe. Or remember."

"Your lost youth?"

"Something like that," Sam says, having lost track of what he meant to say.

"I got plenty of youth to go 'round. Wanna see?" The girl begins to unbutton the fly on her shorts. "I'm not wearing no panties."

"We'll get to that," Sam says. "You got plenty, like you say. It ain't goin' nowhere." *Why am I speaking her language?* "It's a hellava lot easier, don't ya think?" the bedeviller suggests.

"You can't see nothin' driving. Why don't ya pull into one of these empty church parking lots? That would be a good place for us to make it, don't ya think?"

Now she's thinking like me! "I'd just like to watch you make it, you know, by yourself," Sam says.

"Because your mommy told ya that was naughty?"

"I never knew my mother," Sam says blankly. *Again with the honesty. Why is confession so easy here?*

"I hardly did either," says the girl. She pulls off her shorts and skimpy blouse to reveal a lace teddy beneath. She unfastens the crotch snaps. "This sorta takes longer, ya know. It can't be faked. Well, maybe it could be. But you'd know. You're educated." She reaches over and pulls Sam's right hand off the steering wheel readying to use it as a dildo. "I sure would like you to put that tongue you preach with on Sundays someplace soft and then . . ." she keeps up a steady stream of innuendo.

Sam has never heard a woman talk herself through orgasm before.

* * *

THE DIOCESE OF LOS ANGELES
Office of the Bishop
The Rt. Rev. Charles Sprockett, D.D.

November 13, 1990

Dear Mr. Peter White:
Your letter is not being ignored. My difficulty has been finding a time when Deacon Elizabeth Sparks and I can both visit Ascension. I'm happy to say December 4 is fine. Shall we

say 8 p.m., at the home of a vestry member? Please call my secretary with the particulars. I look forward to seeing you. We have some unpleasant issues to face since your congregation cannot sustain a program of the magnitude some may be tempted to consider. Facing the questions of viability will allow us to examine other matters as well. For example, you employ a part-time priest, but allow her to take long vacations in order to reap the equivalent of full-time service when she's with you. This pattern could not continue were you to invest the dollars some apparently believe I should endorse.

Give my best wishes to the members of the vestry.

Sincerely,

Charles Sprockett

* * *

THE DIOCESE OF LOS ANGELES
Office of the Bishop
The Rt. Rev. Charles Sprockett, D.D.

November 13, 1990

Dear Bliss:

I enclose a copy of our letter to your warden. You and I should speak privately before this meeting. I have no intention of letting your vestry go around Elizabeth. She represented my views religiously in her September visit, as your people will soon discover.

But on a personal level, Bliss, I must say I've lost confidence in you. Unless that is rebuilt, I don't see how I can support the rebuilding of Ascension. Let's discuss the changes in your style I feel to be essential, and make them another item on the December 4th agenda.

All I get when I phone you is that blasted answering machine. I can't be leaving messages there. Please call Blanche to firm up a time for us to confer on December 4th. This comes with my best wishes.

Sincerely,

+Charles

* * *

Sprockett's words aren't considerate. But Bliss considers them. She's outraged and she consoles herself, knowing that outrage is entirely appropriate. *Maybe he put no confidence in me in the first place. He's inventing this argument. It's a smoke screen for his decision to choke us on the fumes of our own bier. What sort of 'confidence game' does he want to play? "What hoops would you like me to jump through, sir, to regain your respect?" At what price? And what of the confidence we would like to put in you?*

Nothing would be served, Bliss decides, by her taking a few volleys in private. She never came out ahead in such sessions with her father. Having girded herself she looks at her options. Will tact or intestinal fortitude best serve? Nearly six months have passed and, finally, the fired-up bishop is coming to face Ascension's vestry. They aren't burned-out. They're rising from the ashes with remarkable zeal.

Bliss isn't ready to draft her reply. The Hebrew word for bridge, *geshur*, comes to mind and she decides to go for a drive to look at actual bridges. *Geshur*, she also recalls, implies the hazards of land. Without them, there's no need for a bridge. *My bishop has no confidence in me. He doesn't see that I'm a bridge—with the same qualities good bridges have, strength and expanse.*

* * *

CHURCH OF THE ASCENSION
Spreading the Gospel since 1853

November 21, 1990

Dear Bishop Sprockett,
*   Thank you for your letter of November 13th.*
*   Of course you may share your point of view and elaborate on any subjects you like when you meet with me and the Ascension vestry on December 4th. I don't feel it's necessary for us to take the time for you to share these ideas in advance of the meeting.*
*   It is good for people of faith to agree, but sometimes it's better for them to confront each other in the presence of witnesses when they disagree.*
*   Blessings on you, Bishop Sprockett. May you be upheld in*

all you do to spread the gospel.
Yours truly,
Bliss Bihar Birch

* * *

"Church Doesn't Wait For Walls," Carolyn Banting reporting to *The Los Angeles Times* Thursday, November 29, 1990:
    When a McDonald's in Newport Beach burned last year, it was only five weeks until a smiling Ronald was reopening the eatery, attracting more business than ever. Rebuilding hasn't gone as smoothly for a fire-ravaged church in the barrio.
    Six months ago, when Church of the Ascension's 130-year-old historic building went up in flames, its members hoped to rebuild immediately. That's the way McDonald's does it. Complications getting their insurance settlement and difficulties communicating with the Episcopal hierarchy have slowed them down. They worship in a way that suggests to observers that they've survived a nuclear attack. Members huddle Sunday after Sunday in their tiny "charcoal chapel." It's all that was spared in the Memorial Day weekend blaze.
    Bishop Charles Sprockett has not come to pray with them since the fire. But he will visit next week for a business meeting. Despite their problems, Ascension's parishioners voted last month to give the balance of the monthly operations budget, $998, to a drug rehabilitation program endorsed by the L.A. Police Department.
    According to Warden, Peter White, the church's newest member, a teenager, suggested this charity. White said, "We continue to trust that our life impacts the society around us, whether we hold services in a beautiful church or not." The Church Insurance Corporation will produce its final claim settlement (expected to be about $900,000) before Christmas.

* * *

Sam returns to his morning routine with a certain nostalgia. But he is distracted as he opens his journal. The now-famous novelist Derek Hunter once composed pages *at this very table*. By comparison to Hunter's opus, Sam's output is slender. And nothing has come of it. Presumably, nothing will. Even though Andrea benefited from her exposure to it, in the end, the process always leads back to *this table*.

Sam lays his pen down.

Hunter, whose visit Sam remembers with mixed emotions, came as a tag-along acquaintance of Hannah Thomas, a college chum Bliss had invited. In person, Derek spoke like an outdoorsman. On the page, he favors the wallpaper languages of a myriad modern motel rooms. In a recent Hunter bestseller that Sam tried to read standing up at the bookstore, the author choreographs the Dance of Seventy Veils as he believes it was hoofed and improved upon by the daughter of the New Testament's only female headhunter, Herodias' little Salome.

What Sam envies is Derek Hunter's ability to reveal secrets. He bets on the future—every time. In what seemed a silly piece of writing then, Hunter predicted not only that NASA would find evidence of life on Mars, but that modern spacemen would see angels between here and there. Sam posted a clipping from *Parade Magazine* in his office, reporting that Soviet cosmonauts saw angels flying beside their Soyez capsule. A tidbit of the kind he supposes Hunter continually feasts upon.

"We are carnivores. Of course I will write about you," Derek had told him, grinning. "I'm a flesh-eater. But I can't promise you'll recognize yourself in the disguise I give you. Honestly, I'm much more into the disguise." That remark prompted Sam to look at everything Derek Hunter has written since.

Sam stares at the table.

His morning notebook page remains blank.

Hannah Thomas called one Thursday just before bedtime asking Bliss if it would be all right if she came and stayed for a couple of days. Actually, she asked whether it would be inconvenient for Bliss to take her in, "for a little while." Bliss remembered the woman. Barely. Sam, even then, could only recall three or four of his college friends by name, a realization that was both embarrassing and puzzling. It was only after she arrived that the hosts discovered their guest was traveling with a paramour of no small stature. And where is your husband, Hannah?

"Out of the picture at the moment. We aren't an item," Hannah explained to Bliss at breakfast the first morning, before her friend had finished shaving. "I can't tell you what tomorrow will bring, only that I want to be here to find out. Do I ever." Hannah carried herself like Ruth Gordon and even spoke with the same kinetic voice. A hippie. To Sam, she seemed the personification of a fanciful passion for What Might Have Been. It allowed her to call someone she'd hardly known and sing a few bars of Picking Up Where We Left Off. And, it had worked. Bliss enjoyed Hannah. And Sam was fascinated by the paramour's ability to combine work and pleasure. Not a day went by that Hunter didn't enter several pages into one or more of *his* notebooks.

Sam shifts his gaze to the pages of the still-empty journal.

Hunter read everything in the house. Sam worried faintly that his journals might be seen. And what in their library had elicited the author's praise? "You folks have the finest collection of mid-'70s kiddie lit I've seen," he said without expressing any curiosity as to the whereabouts of children.

Sam had asked him, finally, if he wondered why there wasn't so much as one portrait of a child on the bookshelves.

Derek had tapped his temple. "If I need facts, I invent them."

"How do you do that?" Sam asked.

"If I ask, 'How many calories a day does the Statue of Liberty have to consume to maintain her present weight?' that leads me to wonder, 'How much does she weigh? Who caters to her?' Before you can count the hairs on your chinny chin chin, I've compiled menus for the metal lady for a week and have assigned cooks from seven countries to prepare their best national delicacies for her in the precise quantities she'll require. And I've totaled the grocery bill."

"Ask a silly question," Sam had said in self-deprecation.

"That's pretty much it," Hunter agreed. "You're going to have to excuse me. That one is fresh. I better make some notes. If you ever come across it in print, you can say, 'I was there when he got that Statue of Liberty idea.' People are always asking me where I get my ideas. If you get tired of preaching, I can get you work lecturing on that one." *Did Derek Hunter know I would tire of preaching?*

Sam's notebook remains blank. The unseen forces of the present are slow to whisper messages into this dawn.

Hunter came to hear Sam's homily while Hannah went with Bliss the one Sunday they were in town. Neither had offered reflection on what they'd heard—the very least one might have expected in return for a week's lodging. Chances are, Hunter didn't realize how tenuous Hannah's connection to Bliss was. He likely assumed the women had settled all the hospitality questions. Sam was generous in the latitude he gave the paramour because of his celebrity. Hannah may have come for no other reason than to show off her catch to a woman she'd admired from a distance. Who knew? Refreshed by Hannah's open spirit, neither Sam nor Bliss had spent any time analyzing why the visit had happened. There was nothing annoying about it. Although having company used up a disproportionate share of the food budget, something always reverses expectations where household expenses are concerned. That passes.

What didn't pass was Sam's sense that *his* writing space— *this very table*—had been, in some inexplicable way, sanctified. It was only when Andrea managed to move the locus of the mystery to her office, that Sam took a terrible sabbatical from his ritual. *Andrea broke the spell.*

Sam reaches for his pen.

Andrea's lesson is always the same: that there are choices to be made. Sam feels a new honesty boiling in his blood. *What would I like to know?* he asks himself. And, honestly, he knows that if he could know anything, he'd like nothing better than knowing the whereabouts of that remarkable Thomas woman, Bliss's friend.

Where is she eight years after flaunting her high-spirited self and her not-so-low-key affair in this house? Will Pike and The Seventy deign to consider a minor curiosity? Of course not. So, Sam begins composing without their assistance:

> They met in a bar for the first time the same night she brought him here. *That's right, isn't it? They had a bet, though I don't know which of them won.* For him, it was just another week of staying alive to select the threads of a story. For her, a week she needed to kill. They paraded their affair before us, a couple of perfect strangers. We didn't see through the charade.

It wasn't a charade, is the only thought in Sam's mind when he finishes the paragraph. He sits, neither pondering the idea nor dismissing it, but treating it, rather, like a mantra. *It wasn't a charade.* It gently leads him to a profound silence and to something he has never known.

Sam senses his hand beginning to move across the paper. He

doesn't look down. It's never been like this. Automatic.

13

Holding It Against You

*B*liss rehearsed bringing up the subject of suspected infidelity only to discover she'd rather confront Andrea than Sam. But as the hour for her counseling appointment approaches, she faces an even more urgent personal problem.

"I'm glad you came." Andrea ushers Bliss into her office. "I thought Sam's decision to stop working with me for the time being might also influence you."

Bliss is ready. The rehearsal, a good idea. "Sam doesn't know that I know, *anything*. He accidentally taped a phone conversation he had with you—the one about waiting 'til enough water had gone under the bridge. It ran out the tape on the answering machine, in fact." Bliss flops into her seat. "The hard part was hearing the youth in his voice. I've felt so old lately." Bliss lifts her hands in a gesture of helplessness. "But, hey, I'm getting plenty, you know. Sex, I mean. But the strangest part is, it's *safe* sex. That was my first clue. Sam and I haven't used protection in years."

Andrea hears the unasked question. She waves both hands to ward off the implication. "Bliss, no. It didn't get that far with us."

"Well, good. My need for your help overrides any jealousy. Whatever your impulses were, I can understand them."

"Why are you in such a hurry to forgive?" Andrea asks. "I haven't forgiven myself. Fondling clients isn't what I do. Ordinarily."

"I got caught up in an indiscretion once," Bliss says, "when I was about your age—eight or ten years ago. I've never told Sam. To be honest, the guy still jumpstarts my fantasies."

Andrea nods. "Imagination is a great dildo."

"At the time," Bliss continues, "I didn't even know Derek Hunter. I'd picked up one of his books, but I hadn't read it."

Andrea's tone is not at all professional. "You had *an affair* with Derek Hunter?"

"A fling. Very brief. He came visiting with a college friend who'd apparently intended to show him off as a trophy. But, I didn't catch on. Before long, Derek was taking more interest in adding the hostess to *his* list of conquests. He didn't see himself as my friend's captive. That was my introduction to 'the California lifestyle.' I still can't believe I went along with it."

Andrea gets up to pour herself a glass of water. "I'm in the business of patterns. Not surprises. Your collar suggests certain patterns which the woman in you may, of course, contradict."

"There were women studying at Harvard when I was," Bliss says, "at least one who's a priest now, like me . . ." Bliss accepts a glass of water. "These gals turned tricks in Europe one summer, for 'spending money' they called it. They came back with more cash than if they'd worked summer jobs. And we didn't make a big deal of it. The Church doesn't think to ask nice girls, 'Have you ever prostituted yourself?' It might be different now. I mean, the health risk alone would be unacceptable."

"Were you one of the ones who went to Europe, Bliss?"

"One summer, I did. Yes."

Andrea hesitates. "And did you. . .?"

"No. But I felt as guilty, because I didn't tell my father what I knew." Bliss reaches into her purse and hands Andrea an envelope bearing the seal of the Diocese of Los Angeles. "This came by courier this afternoon. It's what's on my mind."

* * *

THE DIOCESE OF LOS ANGELES
Office of the Bishop
The Rt. Rev. Charles Sprockett, D.D.

February 1, 1991

Dear Sister Bliss,
You've disobeyed my godly admonitions and have acted willfully in a manner unbecoming a member of the clergy. In accordance with the canons, I've appointed three of your peers to examine these charges. They'll decide if a presentment is to be laid against you in order that we may have a timely resolution of

our differences.

The failure of Church of the Ascension to affix a signature to the co-drawn insurance check discredits your leadership. I have no confidence in your ability to steer a congregation, Bliss. It is most regrettable that we may have to resort to an ecclesiastical trial to disentangle this mess.

I remain your brother in Christ.

+Charles

* * *

"This is serious, isn't it?" Andrea says.

"As serious as whether or not I'll be relieved of my duties and deposed. Defrocked, they used to say."

"What's at issue? What discredits your leadership?"

Bliss takes a deep breath. "For you and me, the question is whether I'm holding out for sound reasons. Am I really expressing the wishes of my congregation, or unbeknownst to me, have I simply found a way of manifesting a fight I never had with my father?"

"You're way ahead of me."

"Sprockett might only be a stand in, a straw man, if I'm manipulating my parish to satisfy a power trip of my own ego," Bliss says.

"And what's at issue?"

"The bishop would like to take the $877,000 insurance settlement and make a mark with it in East L.A. He'd like to put a daycare facility or a health clinic, or both, in place under the auspices of the diocese. It sounds noble. And, in his mind, it would show that Episcopalians are concerned for social justice in a meat and potatoes kind of way."

"Doesn't the insurance money *belong* to your church?"

"Yes and no. The hierarchical nature of our organization creates an advise-and-consent situation. Ordinarily, turning over the insurance proceeds to a congregation is a formality. The bishop is supposed to see that no church signs for a mortgage that might fall to other congregations, or the diocese, to repay. In our case, Sprockett's argument is that we only support a half-time priest and many members travel a considerable distance to attend services. So, he sees no reason why we couldn't disband or rebuild someplace where the ground is cheaper. If we'd liquidate our assets and allow ourselves to be absorbed into other congregations, he'd have three million dollars in his social justice kitty overnight."

"I see." Andrea had not grasped the simplest facts of the matter before. "And what do your members think of this scheme?"

"More than half are opposed to disposing of the property. Our parish, more than most, willingly shares its assets. We take our operating balance to zero every month doing community work. We can do that thanks to ongoing endowment income. So the bishop's ideas haven't fallen on deaf ears. But we have to wonder if they're put forward in good faith? He seems to be demanding control. And our national canons are clear that congregations are to retain control of their assets. If the insurance company had sent the check to me saying it required his signature, I'd have sent it back, saying, 'Please reissue this check to the party insured.'"

"But they sent *him* the check?"

"Yes. But it requires *my* signature. I found out it's been on his desk since Thanksgiving. And because we haven't agreed on its disposition, I'm now holding out."

"A stand-off?"

"Totally. And the whole thing is so draining." Bliss slumps in her chair and closes her eyes.

"So what do you need?" Andrea asks.

"Tell me if I'm being obstinate because of an unhealthy obsession."

Without any inflection in her voice, Andrea parrots a reply, "You're being obstinate because of an unhealthy obsession."

Bliss bursts with a belly laugh and Andrea joins her. The hearty release restores each woman to a sense of knowing her own mind.

"I don't think you ever believed you were sick," Andrea says. "You're tired. The kind of tired we mean when we say, sick and tired. If I could wipe your slate clean like a school janitor, I would. Psychologists can improve life in the workplace sometimes by getting workers to apply the secrets of stress management."

"I never think of the Church as a workplace. It's my life," Bliss says. "It isn't a job that's being eroded. And I can't help but think it's the same for Charles Sprockett. He's in a bind. He'd like to dabble in human services. It would make him feel more alive, more socially evolved."

"Isn't he supposed to concern himself with what becomes of you and your church?"

"If Ascension folded, Sprockett probably assumes Sam's parish would hire me part-time. But Sam and I haven't worked together. I'm not sure we're compatible in the *workplace*."

"And what are the chances your peers will recommend that you stand trial?" Andrea hands the letter back to Bliss.

"I can't say. Any number of clergy would need nothing more than a nod from Sprockett to hang me. I've been in the diocese twelve years and some of the old-school clergymen have yet to speak to me. A few even avoid Sam. Politics in church circles is a given. Having a father who landed a cardinal parish, I understand that better than some."

"A cardinal parish?"

"It's what we call those big churches that showcase their senior pastor as having bishop potential. My father stood for election in two other dioceses before he was chosen in Colorado."

"Was he a perfect bishop?"

"He was an old-style bishop. So is Charles Sprockett, though he thinks he isn't. My dad was appalled when I took classes at Episcopal Divinity School at the same time I mastered in history at Harvard. He couldn't bring himself to ask me if I wanted to be ordained."

"Did you?"

"I wanted seminaries to admit women as a matter of course. And I wanted to know what I knew about theology," Bliss says.

"So standing up to a bishop comes as naturally to you as holding your own with your father?"

"Exactly."

Andrea makes another observation. "When the infighting intensifies, you might lose your perspective."

"Yes. I've already lost any respect I had for Charles Sprockett. He takes it upon himself to publish books about women's liberation when I'd rather read women on that subject. I'd prefer to see him empowering the disadvantaged. Granted, he's done that some. I know he isn't simply the ogre he seems to be from my perspective. That's why I worry that this boils down to a personality clash."

"Bliss, I want to ask you something else. Seriously. Would you make a better bishop than he?"

Bliss tries not to block her answer, but she hesitates. "I would.

Yes. But becoming a bishop is a sacramental mystery."

"How so?" Andrea asks.

"It's like finding your mate. We choose to believe that, functioning properly, the Church, with a capital C," Bliss wiggles two fingers on each hand as if putting the C in quotation marks, "embodies the mind of Christ. In other words, its life is guided from a higher plane. A conflict like Charles's and mine could exist to clarify motives, to help a generation redefine its mission."

"You think Christ is behind this?" Andrea sound incredulous. "Does *Christ* endorse his laying these charges against you?"

"The Church *may* be dying. Still, some must go through the process with her. Sound doctrine says no person's ego strength will be substituted for Christ's light in church matters. It has to be okay with me, to endure. To endure even *this*. Circumstance has taken the upper hand and Sprockett wants my parish to absorb the brunt of it."

"I don't like the sound of that. How long does this take?"

"It could be a year until a trial. Then, an appeal. One of the women's ordination trials was won on appeal. This is just so complicating. And with Sam not being himself. I wish he wouldn't avoid coming to you for help right now. I feel more alone than when we lost Sally, and I was never more alone than that."

"All right." Andrea stands because it's time to end. "So let's say next session we tackle the known in this situation, your feelings of loneliness. Perhaps by revisiting the way you handled loneliness before, we can find a better way this time."

Bliss comes and gives her therapist a hug. "Do you really think I let you off too easy, with Sam?"

"If it was me, I would hold it against you," Andrea confesses.

"Well of all people, I understand a strong-willed woman's finding Sam Garland attractive. How can I hold that against you? But, you might help me collect some pointers for not holding it against *him*. I haven't said 'I forgive you' to him." Bliss kisses her own index finger and then touches Andrea's mouth, "Or perhaps it would be better for all concerned if we decide our lips are sealed."

Andrea watches Bliss walk away. *That's the woman I accused of pretending to strengths she doesn't have?*

14

Disarmament & Other Marital Skills

*I*t's Sam's night to cook. "We need to talk," he says to Bliss. His tone is serious. His eyes, intent. But his body, speaking for itself, contradicts him. It leans rakishly against the counter and catches Bliss by the wrist to pull her close.

"Really," Sam says softly, "there's something I need to tell you."

Bliss raises her eyes toward the ceiling. "Is this *something*, something that will lead to our breaking-up housekeeping?"

"Heavens no!"

"Is it something," Bliss continues half-teasing, half-tensed, "that a wife wants to hear?"

"Just let me get this off my chest. I'm ready to say it."

Bliss twists into a tighter embrace, leaning her back into Sam's chest with her cheek touching his. "Seems to me this is what we agreed to pay Andrea Marvin to listen to, 'things a wife doesn't want to hear.'"

At the mention of Andrea's name, Sam pushes Bliss around to face him again, only to discover he would rather not look her in the eye. "Andrea is just the tip of the iceberg," he says looking at Bliss's fingertips and squeezing them. "I've been behaving like an adolescent lately." He lifts her fingers and kisses them.

"Whatever it is, it has made you a spring chicken." Bliss slips her fingers beneath his suit coat, slides them around his waist and then down, locking them onto his buns. Sam returns the gesture and the two hold each other in an embrace that allows plenty of room for the burdens on their chests. It's a strange sight. Two impeccably groomed people in clerical attire joined at the loins.

Bliss slides her hand into Sam's back pocket and fingers the condom in his wallet.

"Don't go seducing me while I'm trying to confess my indiscretions," he complains. "I need to tell you, everything."

"I need a kiss," Bliss answers. Sam obliges. "Keep numbering me among your indiscretions," Bliss says. "I left the man I was planning to marry," she pokes a finger against his chest to punctuate the history lesson, "for you."

"That was years ago."

"If you were to throw me out," Bliss wraps her fingers around Sam's neck, "I believe I would hunt you down where you'd least expect it and beg you in front of God and witnesses to be indiscreet with me, one more time."

Sam is astounded. "Bliss, I'd never throw you out."

"And I can't think of anything short of, say, your announcing you want to court your secretary, that would bring me to even *consider* throwing you out."

"If *you'd* had an affair, you'd want to tell me," Sam says, trying to get his confession on track.

"Would you want me to?"

"That's not the point, Bliss."

"No?" Bliss is unequivocal. "If I'd had an affair, I can assure you, you wouldn't learn of it from *me*."

Sam leads Bliss to the table. He has set it with black plates on white placemats. He strikes a match to light the single candle centerpiece. Wine has been opened and is breathing. Sam's a believer in letting red wine taste the air before he tastes it. He helps Bliss sit and then goes to the oven.

In the teasing tone of a temptress Bliss growls, "Would you like to know whether I've had an affair?"

"No. I just prefer to think you would tell me about your indiscretions if I asked."

"If you asked," Bliss says more seriously, "I think I would try to tell you what you wanted to know."

Sam opens a sack of take-out Chinese food. Singing staples punctuate the silence. Sam reconsiders. "I do wonder, sometimes, I suppose. You have so many interests. *Have* you been indiscreet with anyone besides me these last twenty-four, twenty-five years?" He lifts lemon chicken and beef with broccoli from the sack. He doesn't transfer the food to serving dishes, but goes to the silverware drawer to get serving spoons. He gives Bliss a little pat as he comes around her side of the table and she gets up to shadow him in his last preparation moves.

"If I'm not willing to listen to a litany of your indiscretions, Sam, can't you appreciate that I don't want to itemize mine?" She rubs herself against him. "Can you not just go on living with a woman who keeps secrets?"

"Your faithfulness is no secret," Sam says. "But right now, mine's a sham. I have done those things I ought not to have done."

Bliss cradles his head in her hands. "Sam, none of us is faithful. We've both preached that. I believe it, and I'm sure we can live with it."

"But, Beeb, it's so painful . . ."

"We are forgiven," Bliss says insistently.

"You don't even know what you're forgiving me for!" Sam pulls out her chair again and helps her get seated. He reaches over to the counter and grabs two red cloth napkins before seating himself.

"I wouldn't want to judge you," Bliss tells her mate. "I prefer committing a thousand little indiscretions each time I feast my eyes on you. If you're determined to take us on a guilt trip with all the rights and privileges appertaining thereto, because of some midlife crisis . . ." For years these two have debated when their ardor will slow. Will they conform to statistical norms and register a declining interest in sex in a predictable way? Bliss's hot flashes were the latest test. Each is persuaded their fragile attraction *will* someday wane, and each is surprised when the other is just as willing to cherish this day, sexually, as the day before. It's the stuff of song lyrics. Or, does popular music hymn a truth statistics don't take into account? Love begets love.

Sam sees a smoke screen in place that he hasn't noticed before. "You have had an affair, haven't you?"

"Hardly an affair, Sam." Bliss reaches to take the cashew bits from him to sprinkle on her lemon chicken. "A lapse, a departure from the absolute 'forsaking all others' vow we swore. But, it was a very long time ago." Bliss sees the inquiry in Sam's eyes. "Oh, please," she sounds almost disgusted, "don't make me say it."

"But I want to know, Beeb."

"You think you want to know. Just like a part of me thinks it would be better off knowing who, besides Andrea, you've been indiscreet with." She hides her fear by controlling her voice. It doesn't waiver. This is something she learned watching Donald Birch, the importance of a professional voice. She's grateful it has become second nature to her.

"Who was it? Who did you sleep with?" Sam asks.

In the recesses of her soul, Bliss knows that once the name of a former lover is spoken, it becomes a figment in the imagination of the one you truly hold dear. It can take on a life of its own.

"Take three guesses," Bliss says, almost playfully. She's always tried to be as big as any fantasies she might inspire. Donald showed her that to be powerful one must be mythical in stature.

"C'mon! I don't wanna guess." Sam pouts.

"Why? Prove you believe me." Bliss can feel the momentum shift as cleanly as a tennis ball hit into a difficult place in the opponent's court. A passing shot.

"You haven't had an affair!" Sam practically wails.

"For heaven's sake. I've already confessed. I have. That makes us even. You're trying to confess *something*. And I've let you harass me into confessing *something*. What's the point of bringing names into it?" Bliss says this so matter-of-factly it's apparent she's had time to contemplate her infidelity speech. But Sam only senses the inequality. He's certain he is the greater transgressor. But neither secret, he'd argue, should remain shrouded.

"You already know about Andrea," he points out, to counter her suggestion that names haven't been raised.

"All I know is what you recorded on the answering machine."

"*Did* I?" *Is humiliation to be added to my list of failures?*

"I couldn't bring myself to listen to it all. I fast forwarded and got the idea." Bliss reaches to spoon more lemon sauce over her rice.

"I succumbed to flattery. Andrea had a lapse," he borrows Bliss's word. "But she isn't interested in me. Still, she got me going, and I've taken some foolish chances since. I thought you'd wonder about the condom."

"Are you involved with a parishioner?" Bliss's tone is fraternal rather than accusatory.

"Goodness, no."

"One of my three guesses." Bliss smiles. "I'm relieved."

"I don't want you guessing. Let me get it out and have done with it."

"So, tell me." Bliss puts her fork down abruptly and reaches for a fortune cookie. Cracking it open, she hands the message to Sam.

"Even the Chinese are in cahoots with you," Sam wails. The message Bliss received says, SOMEONE CLOSE WILL TELLS YOU SOMETHING IMPORTANT.

Bliss laughs. "You look fit to be tied with no one to tie you."

Sam smiles. The ungrammatical fortune has persuaded him to reframe his confession. "I want to have you, and hold you, until we are parted by death," he says. He takes the slip of paper and pulls the ends with such force it snaps apart. "You are the most disarming critter on the face of the earth. I don't know how you do it, Beeb, but I'm sitting here getting other ideas."

"Help. Help the Lay Dee," she jokes, pretending that a piece of the ceiling has landed in her lap, "the sky she eez falling." Bliss struggles to her feet. She reaches for her husband's hand. "We can reheat the food. You, I prefer right out of the oven."

15

Adharma & Greed

*A*t her attorney's request, Bliss has come to the diocesan office to try to negotiate a settlement on the disposition of the insurance money. Her other mission is to secure, if possible, a copy of the report Bishop Sprockett received last week from the panel that investigated Bliss's alleged misconduct.

The report lets Bliss off the hook. At least, Ernest Shriver believes it does. He's seen only one page, a page leaked to Sam Garland by someone in his parish.

"You aren't anyone's fool," Elizabeth Sparks says. "You've spent twelve years in a relatively dead-end job. You need a career move. What are you now, fifty-six?"

"Next birthday."

"Well, it would be best if you would begin seeing this situation from both sides, Bliss."

"What constitutes a dead end job is a matter of one's perspective, isn't it? You have, is it, fifteen years on me?"

"Ten," Elizabeth says.

"Yes. You're forty-five. You must realize, Elizabeth, that people see you as having episcopal potential. Bishop Sparks," Bliss lets the impact of the title she's suggesting sink in before she continues. "But instead of qualifying for election by putting in time as a parish rector, you've affiliated yourself *with* a bishop, giving him the best years of your life. You do his research. But your name doesn't appear in his books. And, because you don't serve a congregation, you'll never . . . Well, I've said it."

The urban deacon states the obvious. "My skill doesn't lie with leading congregations, Bliss. Though that's beside the point."

"Not at all. You most assuredly are viewing this fire in a different way than I am. And you have every right to. You're in the employ of the diocese. But please understand why I can't champion the bishop's position," Bliss says.

"Your flock is so small," Elizabeth counters.

"The salt of the earth."

"Haven't they lost their savor?" Elizabeth picks up the biblical counterpoint.

Bliss is agitated. "They've lost their *building*. But in the last ten months, they've proved they can go on being the Church."

Elizabeth responds somberly. "Bliss, we have the legal backing of the chancellor to argue this matter in an ecclesiastical arena."

"Do you also have that recommendation from the trio who investigated me?"

"I wasn't aware you knew of their report. It's just come in and, no, we haven't as yet had a confirmation that a trial is in order. But don't rest easy. Our bishop is a most persuasive man."

"Elizabeth, I'd like to know," Bliss sounds almost amused, "what indictable offence you imagine I'm guilty of?"

"That will be for the officers of the court to determine. But I will say, that your willful failure to co-sign the insurance check is the straw that breaks the camel's back."

"That check," Bliss says, trying to remember her instructions, "has certainly gone stale. I'd have no objection to the proceeds going directly into an account from which neither the diocese nor Ascension can draw until our differences are mediated. Let the national church or a civil court arbitrate. I trust you will pass my conciliatory remarks on. I mean them as *more* than a gesture of goodwill." Bliss stands. "Let's call it, a proposal coming out of this meeting. And, if you'd be so kind as to supply me with a copy of the presbyter's report . . ."

"Hold on. I can't do that." Elizabeth indicates that she'd like Bliss to resume her seat. "I was hoping, before you left, that you'd give me your opinion," Elizabeth fumbles inside her desk, "on some phraseology. Charles's next essay—a speech, actually—to the National Council of Churches board. He's calling it, 'Sweet Sixteen: Women Priests Come of Age on the American Scene.'"

"Elizabeth, you can put whatever words you want to in Bishop Sprockett's mouth about my progress living a priest's life. But the notion that *my kind* have 'come of age'—whatever that means, when *his kind* still have not, is totally offensive. We're in this adventure together. Both genders. Maybe you want my opinion because you entertain some doubts about being the bishop's speech writer. Putting feminist rhetoric in Charles Sprockett's mouth isn't as divine a calling as you may once have thought?"

Bliss heads for the door, but she isn't finished talking. "Let the man speak for himself, why not?" With her back to the urban deacon she bolsters herself to say what she must say. "I'm disappointed you couldn't be more forthright with me about the difficulty the bishop is having conjuring evidence against me." She turns. "You seem to have the ability to be up front. You're the kind of leader I would have hoped to find at my side. But I see that would be asking too much."

"Hold on." Elizabeth gets up. She walks over and puts a hand on Bliss's shoulder. "I respect you. If it could be, you would make as strong a bishop as your father. Certainly a stronger bishop than I could ever hope to be."

"Strength isn't the quality I admire in a bishop," Bliss says. "I want a bishop who remembers his responsibility to act as my pastor. If a bishop is that, he can be forgiven a lot."

Elizabeth looks surprised. "If you've heard the rumor that he's leaving his wife, I can only say, believe it when you see it."

"I hadn't heard that. And if it's supposed to become grist for the mill, you'll have to keep it in circulation. I'm out of the loop. Martyrs aren't supposed to throw themselves to the lions, you know, it takes away the sport."

Elizabeth smiles. "Keep your chin up. Charles may come around when he gets his mind off his own troubles."

"Could we close with a word of prayer?" Bliss asks.

"Certainly."

* * *

Sam hears voices in the living room as he enters the kitchen by the back door. He has two hospital calls to make, but wanted a refreshment stop enroute.

"Sam?" Bliss calls. "Get yourself a coffee and come in. Carolyn Banting, the *Times* reporter, is here."

Bliss has filled their thermos decanter with freshly brewed coffee. Sam puts a teaspoon of Folgers crystals into the bottom of his mug before filling it. He opens the refrigerator and pours a plunk of cream in.

Ms. Banting stands up and reaches to shake his hand. The

reporter is a dark-skinned woman of medium height with fluffy black hair. Her hands, Sam thinks, are rather bony. If she weren't a journalist, she'd likely be a phys ed teacher. But her voice comes out surprisingly high. "We were just discussing the bad ol' days," she says.

"I had to travel on the overnight bus to Cheyenne to preach. And how we thought that was as rough as it would ever get," Bliss says.

Sam looks at Carolyn. "Did she mention she gave them her services for expenses and a dollar a year?"

"No."

"I only went twice a month, on the weekend."

Sam chuckles. He lifts a finger for each day, counting, "Friday, Saturday, Sunday and home again Monday afternoon—the weekend." He waggles the four as contradictory evidence. "We'd promised ourselves we would never spend more than one night apart. With a monumental effort, we stayed faithful to that for a couple months. Winter roads persuaded us to change the vow."

"Do you regret that?" Banting asks.

"Naw. I only regret not having bragging rights." Sam winks at his wife. "We're closing in on eight thousand nights in the same bed. If they aren't entirely consecutive, what's the harm?"

"I can understand Bliss, being born into it," the reporter says, "but Sam, how did you come to get entangled with the church? What got you into the pulpit?"

"Aren't you doing this story on Bliss?"

"How could I leave out her *backbone*?"

"If she's given you that impression, you've let her take you down a garden path. Bliss inherited enough backbone for three priests, maybe three hundred."

The reporter agrees. "Maybe even enough for a bishop. I took the liberty of running her chart. I do character study the old-fashioned way—with the help of an astrology program on the paper's computer. Libra on the ascendant with a Libran moon in the twelfth house gives your Capricorn wife quite an opportunity to tip the balance in favor of the feminine where institutions are concerned."

"Does marriage qualify as an institution?" Sam asks.

"Well, if the truth be known, Bliss looks a bit indecisive in the marriage department. Uranus at one degree Taurus in the seventh house controlled by Aries. I want to find out how you managed to slow her down."

"I dragged her to Yosemite to listen to water and to look at meadows of mountain flowers. Stuff like that," Sam says. "Got her away from the city."

"Was that one of your pleasures? Getting out of town?"

"You're determined to know about me, aren't you?"

"I'm trying to get a picture of the world Bliss is part of," Carolyn insists. "Bliss was telling me about Peter White, her warden. He's taken in a couple of street kids since the fire."

Sam doesn't hide his surprise. "Really?"

Bliss sounds deliberate. "Carolyn's going to contact Peter if she wants his story. I'm just serving as her corroboration on that."

Carolyn is equally surprised. "You two haven't spoken about Mr. White's generosity?"

Sam explains. "We learned long ago that we can't make the lives of each other's parishioners integral to our relationship. We've made some mutual friends who don't worship in either of our congregations and their problems and joys are something we share. But Bliss knows nothing personal about my people. And as to whether or not Peter has a story to tell you, I wouldn't know."

"Bliss," Carolyn says, "perhaps I didn't appreciate the strings you attached to your Gabriel Luna example. I thought I was keeping it in the family. I'm sorry. I'm obliged to keep my promises to sources."

"Always?" Bliss asks.

Carolyn's pen has run dry and she fumbles in the large leather bag at her feet for another. "Occasionally I get information from a semi-reliable source and I have no way to confirm or corroborate it. Say a prostitute spills the names of some of her clients."

It seems to Sam as if Carolyn has chosen a strangely coincidental moment to make eye contact with him.

"I wouldn't treat that as a story, although there might be exceptions. With corroboration from police, the Swaggarts and Jim Bakkers of this world are news. In a smaller arena, there's always another angle to take. I think a reporter has an obligation to go beyond sensationalism." Carolyn pulls a red and brown India-print silk scarf from her bag almost as a magician would. She raises her notebook and drapes the scarf over her knees.

Bliss has a sense that an altar cloth has been laid. *My story is now on her altar. She is the arbiter of what is secret and what is sacred.*

"To me," Sam says coolly, "a reporter's sense of discretion is important. It's a sign of intelligence not to deliberately invade people's privacy." For the first time, Sam feels relieved he didn't tell Bliss everything about his episode with Andrea and his mornings with the street girls. It's easier to think of them as past tense when there's no one who can be wounded by his silence.

"I'll give you an example, Sam," Carolyn says. "Bliss has volunteered that she's seeing a psychologist. I won't print that. Like it or not, some people associate going to a shrink with being unbalanced. To give that impression about your wife would be a miscarriage of justice. But I question whether confidentiality will prevail in the Information Age. People are prone to confession. And you spiritual types, probably more so."

"Even so," Sam says, "my parishioners expect and appreciate my discretion. I don't offer public prayer mentioning names of the sick, unless they specifically ask for it. It's a small thing. And it has come from serving a big congregation. I used to feel quite confident asking a fellow Christian, 'What's the nature of your spiritual discipline?' Now I consider that something to raise only within a small, inner circle."

Carolyn turns to Bliss. "Do you feel that way?"

"With a smaller congregation, we already function as an inner circle. I call it the catacomb mentality."

Carolyn returns her attention to Sam. "May I ask you your own question, in this circle, Sam? What's the nature of *your* spiritual discipline?"

He smiles. "Why don't you see if Bliss can predict my answer to *that* one?"

"Really?" Carolyn is surprised.

"I'll try," Bliss offers. She closes her eyes. "Sam begins and ends every day in the prayerful manner our oldest rubrics suggest. He's very faithful to it. But, in fact, that's the very least of his personal, spiritual discipline." She opens her eyes and continues.

Carolyn hears Bliss say "visionary," and something about Sam's having James Pike not only as a surrogate father, but a mentor. She doesn't fully understand, but she senses that something as intimate as anything that's passed between these two in quite awhile is happening. She can't bring herself to interrupt for clarification. Bliss is radiant. It is as if Sam's wife is speaking in tongues. Carolyn stops taking notes. The atmosphere is charged. Bliss is baring her soul. Sam seems to acknowledge her praise even as he accepts accolades from as far away as angels may rest. The room feels as if it's been rained on, wet with the innocence of unknowing.

Then silence.

Carolyn asks herself, *How can you divorce the message from the messenger? Poem and poet are one. I really must worship again at Ascension.* "Do you two ever bring it home?" she finally asks. "You know, tell each other what you're preaching about, what you think of Bishop Sprockett?"

Bliss and Sam look puzzled.

"All the time," they chime in unison.

"All the time?" Carolyn's echo is tinged with disbelief.

* * *

"Timbers and Tempers Flare," by Carolyn Banting; from a three-part series, *The Los Angeles Times*, Sunday, June 9, 1991:

EAST LOS ANGELES—No one noticed last year on Memorial Day weekend, when flames consumed the dry timbers of Church of the Ascension, the oldest Episcopal structure in Los Angeles.

Now witnesses come forward to describe a new conflagration there. Pride and prejudice rage in a tiny crucible pitting the cathedral-style tactics of the church hierarchy against the catacomb-antics of God's people. The priest in charge of Ascension is under investigation for insubordination. Two months ago, seventy prominent Episcopalians petitioned national officials to scrutinize Bishop Charles Sprockett's handling of the tragedy. They believe L.A.'s metropolitan abused his authority and demanded compliance with his views as a precondition to his signing over the fire insurance proceeds to this small, heritage-conscious congregation.

Sprockett challenges the female rector's oversight unnecessarily, the complainants say. Canon law allows local congregations to make building-related decisions without a bishop's help if no mortgaging is involved. But bishops are required to act as overseers for churches that are insolvent.

Peter White, Ascension's warden, says, "Our rector, the Rev. Bliss Birch, may be taken into ecclesiastical court and put on trial. Her only crime is that she didn't push the *bishop's agenda* down our throats."

Ascension is not insolvent. An endowment fund generates $36,000 a year. The weekly offering is distributed to projects selected by the congregation. Presently, the church is debating dipping into its endowment to hire an architect and retain a lawyer. For the past nine months, the services of Ernest Shriver, senior partner at Thorndike, Shriver and Armacost, have been donated to the parish. Shriver says communication from Bishop Sprockett "shows an appalling lack of concern for the will of the congregation."

Sprockett hasn't said who investigated the alleged ecclesiastical sin of Ascension's rector. "That report came to the Standing Committee and then was sealed," he told the *Times*. Shriver speculates, "You act on a report that shows cause, and seal one that doesn't. The chancellor can take only so many liberties in interpreting canon law."

Bishop Sprockett is taking a summer sabbatical to write his seventh book, *Adharma*. Adharma is a Sanskrit word meaning, "individual disharmony with the nature of things." The Standing Committee is authorized to carry forward his agenda in his absence.

* * *

THE DIOCESE OF LOS ANGELES
Office of the Bishop
The Rt. Rev. Charles Sprockett, D.D.

June 14, 1991

To All Clergy:
Friends,
Thanks to the priest at Church of the Ascension, a handful of her parishioners and her flamboyant counsel (who has compared our in-house struggle to the Gulf War), I feel comment from this vantage is now appropriate.
Ascension has forty communicants. Forty! The church has

not paid its full assessment in years. The congregation is shrinking. That is cause for legitimate concern. Future growth at the present site is unlikely. Meanwhile, the land is worth a million dollars. And the insurance settlement when it finally came in was just under $900,000.

When Ascension was destroyed, it was our conclusion it wouldn't be in the best interests of the Episcopal Church to hand over sole control for rebuilding to her fragile and far-flung membership. These days, $900,000 buys a church that seats 200 to 500 people, not 40. We initiated discussions with the rector and her vestry. These immediately broke down. Chancellor Averill Cunningham has suggested that Ascension, in its present state, has reverted to mission status and must seek our assistance. I find this a compelling argument. And I have added Ascension to the "endangered churches" list.

I asked the Church Insurance Corporation to draw a two-party settlement. That was no problem. It's their policy to do so in cases involving near total destruction. Ascension's lawyer forced the national church to appoint an expensive panel to review my so-called harassment of this congregation. This happened only after I appointed three presbyters to look into Ms. Birch's possible ecclesial misconduct in failing to co-sign the check we received last November.

Today, I propose to deposit the disputed monies in a jointly held account until Ascension draws up plans that address our concerns. To date, they still have not co-signed the check. It is our wish to cooperate with the faithful members of Ascension. We will not, however, abrogate our episcopal responsibility. As I will be unavailable later (having accepted an invitation to visit and lecture in Japan at the conclusion of my sabbatical), I felt you deserved a few words concerning this "burning question" from the horse's mouth.

Have a good summer.

+Charles

Los Angeles

16

Showing a Goddess Some Respect

//Why did I summon you?" Ernest Shriver asks Bliss jovially as he closes the door behind her. He walks to his desk. "Shriving has fallen on hard times," he says. With a Grouchoesque mannerism, he taps an invisible cigar to dislodge an imaginary chunk of ash. He lifts the fire-maker to his lips again. Pinkie extended, Shriver wiggles the unseen object. Bliss recalls the after-dinner smell in her grandparents' cabin on summer evenings forty years ago. Strangely, Shriver's office has a sensate just-been-smoked-in smell.

This is only the second time lawyer and client have met face to face, though they speak on the phone frequently. Shriver, sixty-four, has twice served on national church committees with Bliss's father. Though Bliss is not even ten years his junior, Ernest feels very fatherly towards her. He's been a laid back, Type B kind of guy since before the label was invented. He's not afraid to carry props into court, and he views the proceedings there rather like a movie in which he's asked to appear.

"Shriving?" Bliss has forgotten what the name Shriver implies.

"Confession." He takes another drag on his pretend weed. "I'm making a pitch to protect my ass. I hope you don't mind my speaking freely." Ernest doesn't wait for a response. "I respect you, and I don't want you thinking I'm an idiot when I go to bat for you."

"You're in no danger of that," Bliss assures him.

"Maybe. Maybe not. I want to be sure you understand the strategy we've targeted," Ernest says. "I need to know you've agreed to follow it."

Bliss leans forward. She puts her elbows on the edge of Ernest's desk and repeats what they've previously discussed. "We aren't going for a win up front. That would be naive. We just want to build a case that we can win on appeal."

"Exactly."

Bliss has been absorbing the meaning of this tack, steeling herself for the inevitable. Charles Sprockett will remove her as the rector of Ascension. Or since he maintains it's now a dependent mission, he'll discharge her as its vicar. Either way, her imminent removal is as certain as sunrise.

Ernest makes eye contact to repeat something he's said on the phone. "We find ourselves in a no-win situation at the moment. They've got the court stacked against us. But that should only compound its propensity to err. And error will insure a prompt reversal once we bounce this up to the appeals level. Bliss, I've already received two amendments to the charges filed against you. I don't suppose we'll know precisely what Cunning Ham is accusing you of until we get into court. Disclosure is a civil amenity the ecclesiastical court can overlook. Did you know," Ernest says with a change of tone and a bemused smile, "Joan of Arc faced seventy charges at first? By the time they got to trial, they'd boiled them down to twelve."

"How can you remember that?" Bliss asks.

"Easy. Septuagint and disciples. Who can forget such biblical numbers? Meanwhile, our own harassment case is pending. If the national panel finds insufficient evidence of Sprockett's misconduct, they may still open the door to a civil action. A damages suit." Ernest is on a roll. "Try as we might, Sprockett is not going to testify at your trial. But we may be able to put him on the stand in another venue. I've taken the liberty of drawing up a complaint for you to sign. I'll file it if, or rather, *when* Sprockett moves to relieve you of your priestly duties."

Bliss takes the document and reaches into her purse for a pen. "By the way," she pulls out an envelope and lays it on Ernest's desk, "my vestry has authorized me to retain Thorndike, Shriver & Armacost. Here's $50,000. We managed to withdraw this twenty-four hours before the chancellor asserted diocesan control over our assets."

"Bravo." Ernest fingers the certified check. "The partners will be pleased. Of course, we aren't worried. You Ascension folks have all kinds of capital. The better part, at the moment, frozen by fire." He waves the imaginary cigar across his desk.

Bliss smiles and repeats the punch line, "frozen by fire." She looks over the complaint: Sprockett wrongfully declared Church of the Ascension "extinct" to gain control of its endowment, exercised powers reserved to the congregation and violated church law that bishops are pledged to uphold. Bliss recognizes what she's been outlining for Shriver, even in legalese.

"What's the legal meaning of 'extinct?'" she asks.

"The California Code uses that term to describe an organization which ceases to function. Like the dinosaurs." Shriver crosses to his bookshelf and flips through a text. "Like hallucigenia, here. Don't you love her name? She's just a fossil, don't get around much anymore." Ernest brings the book over. "What Sprockett succeeded in getting the Standing Committee to do when it declared that Ascension be treated *as* a mission, was to make the *parish* extinct. It's a fossil rather than a breathing being. While Ascension still considers itself a living life form, the bishop says, no, you're actually a dead one. Charles Sprockett is like a grandstanding palaeontologist asserting that a certain critter was *never* capable of swimming upstream."

Bliss closes the book on Shriver's diagrams.

"In some circumstances," Ernest says in a conciliatory tone, "that assertion would be appropriate. If your parish *were* dead, or if your group fit the definition of a mission. But it doesn't. If I can subpoena the Standing Committee's minutes, I believe I can prove people knew, *even as they were voting*, that Ascension is *not* a mission. Missions don't have endowments and $900,000 worth of insurance owing to them. They don't sit on a million dollars worth of unmortgaged property."

Bliss signs the complaint and gives it to Ernest. "It was the ground as much as the check that flagged attention. You're right."

"Now, I have something for *you*," Ernest says. The white-haired lawyer reaches into the top drawer of his desk and brings out a black leather bag. From it, he extracts a camera lens which he puts back in the drawer; the bag, he passes to Bliss. "I want you to bring this each day of the trial." He acknowledges her curious look. "When I feel we've gotten something on the record that will be beneficial on appeal, I'll slip you one of these." Shriver displays a white marble between his thumb and forefinger. "We'll need a dozen in the bag in order to have the makings of a good appeals brief. You'll know where I think we stand, moment to moment."

Bliss is delighted. "A code."

"In my teens, I had a diction teacher who made me speak with marbles in my mouth. You know this. Just like the joke, but it really happened. Each session, she'd have me speak with one less marble. By the end, even with a couple marbles, I sounded fine. And she actually told me," he raises his hand as if swearing, "Ernie, when you've lost all your marbles, you'll be a world class speaker."

Bliss laughs. "You really had that teacher?"

"Yes. And I remember a candle. She'd measure the distance you could bring your lips back from the flame and still extinguish it by projecting certain consonants. Power," Ernest says, exaggerating the explosiveness of the P. "She used to say she wouldn't pass a man until his *bite* was as good as his *bark*." Ernest rolls the white marble across the desk so slowly Bliss is able to open the little bag and have it ready.

"We have one in the bag?"

"Yep." Shriver stands and paces as he explains. Bliss imagines that this is the way she will see him in the cathedral when it's converted into a courtroom next month. "The assessor appointed to give legal advice to this court doesn't pass muster. She's a fine lawyer and a confirmed Episcopalian," Shriver says, "but she was *not* elected. Rose Hastings was hastily appointed to her post the day the bishop returned from his diocese-funded goodwill tour of Japan. And she will doubtless be confirmed by his hip pocket Standing Committee. She'll serve all by her lonesome, though our canons clearly state an ecclesiastical court must have three assessors."

Ernest turns toward Bliss. "I probably won't say things like 'that hip pocket Standing Committee' when we're at trial, but just remember, it doesn't hurt our strategy one bit if I do."

Bliss nods.

Ernest lifts his foot onto the low window ledge and takes in his 180-degree view of the city skyline, much changed in the twenty-five years he's practiced law out of this downtown building. "That irregularity, just an iota of impropriety, you might say, is magnified by the fact that Rose Hastings is one of those persons who administers the monies held in trust by the diocese. As of now, that includes Ascension's funds. Without question, she should step down. But, she won't recuse herself. So you have a marble, and we'll get good mileage out of it in on appeal. Okay, Bliss, let me hear your explanation of where we stand," Ernest directs.

Bliss pops the little marble out of the bag and inspects it as if looking for a flaw. "All the legal advice the panel of judges convening this court receives comes from a woman who should have known she has no business serving in the position."

Ernest nods. "Good. The conflict of interest has been called to Rose's attention by none other than Yours Truly. She's failed to seek any remedy. But I don't think she's a glory seeker. Her firm is well connected. If she'd wanted to, Rose Hastings could have litigated nothing but cases involving the rich and famous. Instead, she's taken some unpopular cases. I give her that."

"So?"

"So, she's been drawn into that vortex, that core of bright thinkers our bishop attracts. We used to call charm like that charisma. Now charismatic means those people who sing ditties with their hands raised over their heads." Ernest has lifted his own hands in the air. Clearly, he could have died happy without seeing *his* church take on the gestures of the evangelical sectors of Anglicanism.

Bliss lets *Rose* drop back into the pouch. "Eleven to go. Like launching a rocket." She squeezes the sack, manipulating the occupant of the bag around, imagining the tiny sound that will be generated when it is joined by another. And another, until a full complement of Shriver's unique amphictyony is in the bag.

Shriver watches, pleased with himself for creating a perfect distraction for his client. "If our bishop weren't in such a god-awful hurry to make an example of you," he says, "he could have waited until the annual convention. We could have elected the assessors that the canons require." Ernest turns back to his cityscape. From this window, he can see the crown of the sand-colored Episcopal cathedral. "Charles Sprockett is a wise young ruler, but he's overlooked one very important thing, in my book."

"What's that, Ernest?"

"The least of these. Doesn't the Bible say, 'inasmuch as ye have done it unto the least of these, my brethren, ye have done it unto me?'"

"You remember your King James," Bliss says. "Can I ask you something?"

"Shoot."

She sounds more childlike. "How do you know what to do?

I mean, ecclesiastical trials are rare."

"Ecclesiastical tribunals know nothing of the Throne of Grace, I'm afraid. They take their cue from civil procedures. And there are precedents. The 1975 trials in Ohio and Washington, D.C., determined the fate of the men who allowed the women ordained in Philadelphia to visit and administer communion in their parishes. You could say we're seeking the same hand dealt Peter Beebe in Ohio. His conviction was overturned on appeal."

Bliss knows what became of Peter Beebe. Although exonerated, he left the priesthood. With as little as two weeks left to her to function as priest-in-charge at Ascension, Bliss is loath to consider that *her* days in the priesthood may be numbered. Comparisons with Joan of Arc, facetious as they may be, are easier to take than this comparison to Beebe. How ironic that his name is pronounced, like her nickname, Beebee. A court at the turn of the millennium is not going to mete out a burning at the stake penalty. But figurative death, like Beebe's, is terrible to contemplate. It is so much more likely to happen. If your career goes up in smoke, it doesn't much matter that, in the end, the smoke was only figurative.

"It's my turn," Bliss says.

Ernest assents. He sees the clergywoman's determination. She'll be as tough as nails in the courtroom. That will give him all the latitude he could want. Knowing you can't throw your client a curve allows you to cut a wide swath.

"I'm glad we understand each other," he says. And no sooner are the words out of his mouth than Ernest Shriver realizes, *You may understand me better. But will I ever understand you? You look like a prom queen and think like a goddess. Can't we treat you with the respect you deserve?*

* * *

Pasadena: November 4, 1991

Donald Birch is seated beside his daughter at the defense table facing the long judges' bench on the platform. "There must be forty cameras pointed at us," he says. Donald rocks back and forth in his seat, his spider-long legs astride the chair as if it were a saddle. He looks like a boy bored by the wait.

The prosecution table is across the center aisle. *On the bride's side,* Bliss thinks. Averill Cunningham, the Church Advocate, has a stack of exhibits that his only witness will explain.

Only last week the trial site was moved from downtown to All Saints, Pasadena. This church is to Sam's, what East L.A.'s Epiphany is to Ascension, the more colorful baby sister. Interesting things are always on tap at All Saints, like at All Souls. But All Saints is decidedly liberal. In the '60s, guitar masses here brought in the crowds. Ten weeks from now, hundreds will come to see two men exchange wedding vows—a test case. But today, the event of interest is an ecclesiastical trial. This venue saves Bliss two hours' driving time, but that consideration didn't prompt the switch. Chancellor Cunningham suggested the trial not be held in close proximity to diocesan headquarters. Access to Bishop Sprockett might prove too great a temptation for a court sitting downtown.

Bishop Birch came from Florida three days ago. He announced his travel plans before Bliss could invite him. And that pleases her. The desirability of his *charismatic* presence was apparently on both their minds.

Bliss nods toward the photographers. "What do they expect? I feel like a character in a mystery play. What newsworthy thing can be generated by watching a handful of infighting church fanatics? If this were a board game, I'd be your basic Sacrificial Lamb."

"But a very photogenic one," Donald says in a stage whisper. "Beautiful people look good even if they're being crucified. It's a great lead-in to the local news. The still photographers are presetting their F stops. Gonna push their film to 25,000 ASA, I'd bet. In the paper, you'll look like medieval mosaic."

Carolyn Banting, who has overheard the bishop's comment, chuckles. She and Bliss exchange a smile. Bliss thinks it's ironic that Carolyn's taking an interest in this story may have been one of the things that kept the pressure on those who subsequently argued in favor of staging this tribunal.

"The *real* trial isn't going on the record," Bliss says absently to her father.

"Thinking about what you have to say?" Donald asks.

"Thinking about what I *shouldn't* say."

"Clearing the cobwebs," he confirms. "I usually recite scripture under my breath to do that. The 23rd Psalm works pretty well."

"Thank you." But instead of contemplating the good shepherd, Bliss drifts to a scene from a recent dream she had. Joan of Arc was asleep in her dreary cell and, like Bliss, dreaming. Somehow, Bliss knew Joan was dreaming of her, a woman more statuesque and blonde, facing ecclesiastical censure in the future. The first question came, "Do you feel we've jumped to conclusions?"

And Bliss heard herself answering in Joan's dream. "That's all we know how to do. The Shroud of Turin is debunked and no one thinks to ask, who was the genius, then, who painted it? What was the artist's intent? Where is mystery? Only in something science hasn't explained to our satisfaction yet?"

"Is there something we haven't explained to your satisfaction?" the inquisitor asks.

"The Lakota people have a word, *wasi'chu*, which tells you what my parish is enduring. It means, *the one who eats all the fat.* Wasi'chu became synonymous with land-grabbing colonizer."

Bliss snaps out of her reverie marveling that she can recall the dream and wondering if it's true that the Lakota labeled the colonialists. "Dad? Did I have strange dreams as a kid?"

"Don't you remember the time you told us you'd been in a phone booth all night?"

"What was the problem? Isn't that every teen's dream?"

"You knew exactly what the problem was. You hadn't been able to reach the party you were calling, because you were . . ." Donald works to drag the memory out of her.

"Dialing from the wrong side of the page," they say together.

"The 23rd Psalm is better than an old phone book," Donald says, patting his daughter's shoulder and bending to kiss her cheek.

Saint Joan is trying to rollover in her sleep. But the handcuff attaching the frail woman to the cell wall prevents her from completing the move. The prisoner can find no comfort. Bliss, the future visitor on hand, lifts a necklace from around her own neck. She drops its crystalline circlet—encasing a bright, holographic butterfly—into the lock on Joan's shackles. Although the *key* appears to fit, it won't trip the lock. Bliss tries it at the other end where the chain attaches to the wall. There, the lock springs open. Joan, still cuffed and asleep, rolls over onto the chain. Her ribs will be bruised in the morning.

"Humanity is made to mirror God, male *and* female," Joan hears the fair-haired New World woman saying. "A wonderful picture of the godhead comes from the Lepcha people of Central Asia. They credit a husband and wife as co-creators of the world. Theirs wasn't a marriage made *in heaven*, but rather the marriage which *made* the heavens."

"We aren't here to lend credence to primitive dogma," announces the inquisitor in Joan's dream.

"And why not if it's a finer revelation than our own?" Joan retorts. "In its way, our own scripture affirms the Lepcha's understanding."

Bliss resumes her argumentation, "If the Holy Imagination forgot itself and manifested for a thousand years almost exclusively as past tense male, we *must* restore the present tense feminine if we would speak faithfully of God's glory. Why would only half of all creation be labeled good? God saw it all. And it was *all* good for something."

Sam Garland, in his role as assistant press officer, shows reporters to their seats and shoos the photographers to a standing room only area on the font side of the crossing.

Bliss hears a door slam. Her father takes her by the elbow and lifts her to her feet. Ernest, at her other side, lets his fingers drag on the table. He looks as if he's about to tease music from the keys of an unseen piano.

Five black robed judges enter and everyone else rises. A few butterflies leave their perches in Bliss's stomach to test their wings. They move closer to her heart. She looks to her father who returns her gaze with an intensity she welcomes. The impatient boy rocking on his chair has gone to his room; the man with enough backbone for forty stands with her. *This is it*, she realizes, *I'm standing trial.*

* * *

Ernest Shriver finds moments for wedging comic relief into the preliminaries. "Chairman Comanito, didn't Mr. Cunning Ham, himself the Church Advocate in this case, suggest to you that the Ascension Church monies now held in trust, be invested in interest-bearing accounts?"

"He did."

"And as head of the Standing Committee, didn't you personally see to it that those monies *were* so invested?"

"I did."

The presiding judge interrupts, "Counselor, is this relevant?"

"I'm establishing, for the record, Mr. President, that this witness, the *only* witness appearing for the prosecution, is a common usurer. In the event a juror in a higher court has Muslim leanings, everything in this witness's testimony will be deemed inadmissible by reason of his indulgence in a corrupt, profit-taking practice. I thought it a much easier point to establish, Your Honor, than whether or not the gentleman is engaged in the unholy practice of breeding mules."

"Might I remind you that you're sorely testing the patience of this court, Mr. Shriver?"

"I can see that. And frankly, that was my intent. Thank you. My client is quite familiar with the development and testing of patience. A taste of how that feels might improve this panel's sympathy for her."

"And perhaps it won't," the presiding judge answers coolly.

"Right." Ernest digs into his pockets and winks at Bliss. "I must not have all my marbles."

17

This Can't Be Happening

*T*angled into hundreds of pages of testimony, one question formulates itself again and again, "Why did God allow Church of the Ascension to burn in the first place?" Ernest Shriver has seen to it.

The Church Advocate harps on his favorite "why" question, as well. "Why did the accused rush to obtain the aid of a renowned litigator instead of turning to her bishop for help as she pledged in her ordination vows to do?"

After several days, when it is finally time to stage the defense, Shriver tells his client, "We're bringing her home, like a carnival heading south for the winter. Give 'er all you've got, my dear." An adrenaline rush lifts Bliss. After a moment of pure exhilaration, she wonders, *How can I be happy at a time like this?* That's when she notices a new member in the press corps. *Why didn't Sam tell me he was coming?* Larger than life in the media section wearing togs fit for a safari sits Derek Hunter. Hunter Thompson might have seemed a more likely investigator. But out of nowhere the novelist is here.

Bliss feels a hand on her shoulder. "I only applied for credentials this morning," Derek explains, after catching up to the accused and her father in a back corridor on their way to lunch.

Bliss introduces the writer to Donald Birch who seems unfamiliar with his reputation.

"You know," Derek says, "I never put three good sentences together without remembering your explanation of the trinity— light, love and laughter. I carry those words. The Father of Light, a pillar beside the understanding Mother of the Son of Love, who rejoices in the Spirit of Laughter." He taps his chest. Seeing tears on Bliss's cheek, he says, "I'm sorry," and pulls a handkerchief from one of the many pockets on his vest.

"Anything gentle simply reduces me to tears these days, I'm afraid. I'm trying not to take things personally. But, it's hard. I would say, *damned hard*, but a girl thinks twice before swearing in front of her father." She puts an arm around Donald and gives him a squeeze. "I guess you can take it." He smiles.

"I don't mean to make it any harder," Derek Hunter says. "But drama like this happens ... well, it hasn't been staged in five hundred years. And they made a saint of the last woman we put through this, you know." Derek then slips his arm about Bliss's waist and adds quietly, "You've always struck me as saint material. How soon 'til you testify?"

Bliss shrugs. She looks up at her dad and jokes. "Writers! They're incorrigible vampires looking for fresh blood." She checks to see if Derek is smiling. He is.

"Can we do lunch?" Derek asks.

"I don't think so," Bliss says. "Sam's meeting us. We set up this rendezvous, ironically enough, to *avoid* the press. Of course, it's hard to think of you as *the press* ."

"Sir," Derek says to Donald, "I'm going to whisk your daughter into this classroom. If you'd be so kind as to give us a knock when Sam gets here?"

Donald hesitates, but the deed is done.

As soon as the Sunday School room door closes, Derek pulls Bliss into his arms. She raises a finger against his lips. Her mind resists being swept up, but another mind urges her to step on the gas pedal, the way you do when you're in sight of home after a long trip. She withdraws her protesting finger from Derek's lips, and he says, "I couldn't let you cross these coals alone. I had to come. We are kith." She is all he remembered, and he waits for the inevitable.

Bliss holds him. She feels the urgency in his body. It's an invasive, youthful energy. The difference in their ages didn't seem to matter ten years ago, and in her fantasies it never matters. In the flesh, however, the unbridledness of him is alarming. "I'm not sure," she says.

"They could strip you of your priesthood, couldn't they?" He moves himself gently against her and slides his hands down her arms, around onto her back, and down. Slower than any sex or dancing, the gestures convey a desire he doesn't put into words.

Despite her sense of alarm, Bliss's body answers his, gesture for gesture; speaking to his arms, pulling him closer. *Welcome home.* "They can *try*, yes. The bishop has already issued an injunction against my functioning as a priest. I can't officiate at mass again for two years unless I'm exonerated. And winning that here isn't possible. But, my case *is* going to be won, Derek. On appeal. Keep your eye on the white marbles."

"They mean something?"

"The two this morning are new matters on the record that Shriver feels improve our appeals case. But I haven't asked him what they are yet."

"And you've got others in that black pouch?"

"Oh, yes. One represents the judge sitting at the far end. He should have disqualified himself. Conflict of interest. He serves on a panel responsible for investing money the diocese holds in trust. So does the woman advising this court."

"It took Shaw to defend St. Joan. St. Bliss can at least fire up *this* literary intelligence against her detractors."

"Sweet. But aren't you the guy who said you get your characters out of the blue?"

"It *looks* like they're from out of the blue. But every red flag I wave and every white lie I tell has circulated in somebody's bloodstream. All the important things are of the flesh. Like with us. With kith." He pulls closer and whispers, "That's a soul mate's salute. I'm sure the better angels of our nature will bring us to each other again, in the last twilight. We greeted the dawn of eternity together. I believe that." He looks deep into her eyes. "You are flesh of my flesh. Knowing that, keeps me going." He nuzzles against her neck.

Bliss accepts a kiss before stepping back from the dance. Derek sees that she isn't going to allow him this close again, temporal vows meaning what they do to her.

"How are your kids, Derek?"

He steps around behind her and massages her shoulders as he recites the accomplishments of his sons. "The oldest is in his last year of college, a communications major, with hopes of making it in the Giants' organization. He'll play in Everett this summer. The youngest is a senior in high school. They are both on the brink, brimful of enthusiasms. I suspect my oldest boy has fathered a couple of bastards since leaving his mother's house."

"Really?"

"Well, he shows that he inherited his old man's hankering flank. And I don't say that proudly. In my case, it's that I never met a woman I could be faithful to who hadn't already made her promises to someone else."

Bliss turns to face him. "It would relieve my mind to know you *don't* count me among those you think you could have been faithful to," she says.

"I'd do almost anything to relieve your mind," he takes her hand as if he might kiss the back of it, "but I've given up lying. You are a throwback, you know? You remind us of rituals that fall millennia apart, the return of the Sister Bride. You must be an old soul to have acquired such patience."

"And such truthful kith."

Derek Hunter isn't sure that Bliss's recognition is fully awakened. But even if her response is only intuitive, he is heartened. He bends to kiss the tips of her fingers.

There's a rap on the door.

"You're an old soul yourself, walking the poet's path to Wisdom. You know what's best left unsaid." And then Bliss reaches to open the door.

* * *

"If I didn't know better," Donald Birch wants to make small talk over lunch, "I'd say your writer friend has more than a casual interest in you. He's an adventurer looking for an adventure."

Bliss looks to her husband.

"Derek Hunter spent a week vacationing in our home once, almost by accident," Sam says. "He came with one of Bliss's college friends. I tell myself Mr. Hunter used the two of us as inspiration for his novel, *Forsaking All Others*." Sam slides closer to Bliss.

"I was surprised to see him," Bliss says. She's decided to ignore, for now, Sam's inventing a title that is *not* in Derek Hunter's opus. Every title Hunter *has* written is shelved in the guest bedroom Donald Birch presently occupies.

Sam goes on. "You couldn't have been more surprised than I. He just appeared this morning asking for credentials. Since we had plenty of press packets left, I saw no reason to deny him. I pointed out that he could watch just as well from the observers sections, but he wanted access to the media room."

"No harm." Bliss fumbles under the table to find Sam's knee. *"Forsaking All Others?"* she asks, giving it a squeeze.

"A work-in-progress." Sam gives Bliss a quick kiss.

"Did you expect us to get further this morning?" Donald asks his daughter.

"No. Ernest has always said our case will take days and possibly weeks to present. I was only surprised the judges insisted upon writing their responses to his voire dire. They must see themselves as under the gun."

Sam brightens. "As well they should. Everyone can see they've decided to convict you."

"If they can't hide that, so much the better," Bliss says.

"Your bishop," Donald says, "has been careful. Hasty, but careful. The court president is clean. Squeaky clean. It will add time to the proceedings, but by having a minority-view justice running the whole sheebang, the veneer of fair play is intact. Cunning. The same way he removed Sam by appointing him to work with the press. Clever. I'm so glad I came. You really need me."

"I do."

Donald cocks his head to one side. "You know, I shouldn't even be here. I died over a year ago."

Sam's ears perk up. "Died? Last year?"

"A Sunday, it was. At an evangelism rally. Their wrap-up luncheon pretty near wrapped *me* up. Something was stuck in my throat and, like an idiot, I stepped out into the hall to take care of it myself. There wasn't anyone to see, and I was choking. I collapsed. Like they say, I saw things from above. I was, you know, floating. I could see the banquet room as well as the hallway. If this nice woman priest hadn't come my way from the ladies room, I'd have been a goner. So I get this feeling sometimes now, of living on borrowed time. If there's a reason I was spared, maybe this is it, Beebee. Being here. With you."

Sam's curiosity hasn't been satisfied. "So, this woman came along and revived you right there?"

"Oh, no. An ambulance was called and they took me in to Emergency. I saw all that, too. I tell you, I thought for sure I was dying. I even heard Betsy calling. But I wasn't able to see her. It was quite a shock when I found myself back in my body with this terrible pain in my throat."

"You didn't tell us!" Bliss reprimands.

"In the end, it was nothing. I was perfectly okay. You and I probably didn't talk for a week. It slipped my mind, maybe. I dunno. It would have been a fine way to go, I'll say that. Fast. Clean."

"Papa!"

Sam laughs. "Bliss wants to be kept apprised of your near misses."

"When you get to this age, you don't think so much about dodging the bullets," Donald says. "Isn't that what St. Paul says, *Think of me as dead already. I'm just here as an angel of the Church*?"

Sam ponders his father-in-law's confession. The old Donald did die. And this one is so much more congenial.

* * *

"I call Gabriel Luna to the stand." Ernest Shriver's voice rings in the All Saints' chancel.

"Gabriel Luna. If you are present, please come to the stand," the court president announces. The phrase, "if you are present" has been added to the refrain ever since the bishop and no member of the Standing Committee came forward when Ernest Shriver first cast about for witnesses to corroborate or challenge Hugh Comanito's testimony.

Bliss sits taller. She is aware of having no expectations. Other parts of this proceeding have played in her dreams and have seemed surreal when they actually took place. But this witness has not come forward in her nocturnal anticipations. She has no sense of recollection about what is happening. It is fresh.

Gabriel Luna comes down the aisle slowly. The Mexican-American teenager is big, big in the way Hawaiian men are big. There's no place on his body that seems angular. He is defined by a series of gentle curves. His eyes slope downward giving the impression he's just been awakened. His lips are as broad above as below, colored a shade of brown slightly darker than his face, but no match for his sparkling, nearly black eyes or dramatic black brows.

Bliss feels an inner excitement. Carolyn Banting smiles at the novelist seated beside her. He's begun jotting his impressions stream-of-consciousness fashion. Carolyn already has the story of Gabriel's finding a home with Peter White in the bag. His appearance here only heightens her prospects for telling it.

"State your name, please," Ernest Shriver says.

"Gabriel Roberto Julio Enrico Luna. I'm called Gabe, or Gabriel."

"One of the reasons I've called you to testify before this court, Mr. Luna, is that you recently became a member of Church of the Ascension where my client served as priest until her inhibition, is that not true?"

"She was there last Sunday, like the rest of us," Gabe says.

Ernest shakes his head as if unlearning something. "Did Ms. Birch celebrate the Eucharist there last Sunday?"

"Up in front? No. The bishop won't let her do that now. Not until this trial is over, if it says she is not guilty. Otherwise, not for two years. You know. We got a letter. I really don't know why the bishop is fighting with us. It is hard to understand."

"How long have you been attending Church of the Ascension, Gabe?"

"Well, I don't know how to count it. I used to come some on my own before I met Peter, Mr. White. And now, maybe nearly a year it is, I'm going on Sundays like everybody else."

"Are you the only new member of the congregation?" Ernest asks.

"No. My friend Sonny. He is going since the fire, like me. And there is a family. They transferred from being, Methodists I think it was. Everyone else in my family is Catholic. But I don't have to transfer no papers. Sister Birch just went and had a talk with my mother. The Sister, she knows some Spanish, a little, and that helps when she wants to know about my baptism and that kind of thing."

"There's another important reason I asked you to testify today besides establishing the fact that people have joined the church despite its tragedy. Do you recall our discussion about the evidence you could give?"

"Yes."

"Would you go ahead, then? Where were you the night Church of the Ascension burned?" Bliss leans forward and Carolyn Banting flips over a page in her notebook.

"That was a night when most of Menudo was on the streets pushing. But I wasn't. I wasn't pushing because I'd been given the job of pony. I'd done that, and I was just staying out of the way.

Letting things happen. One of my favorite places to go to stay outta the way, back then, was at Ascension in the back row by the window of the guy who wrote his revelations. I think he is called St. John, the Divine. They saved that window after the fire and a couple of others, too."

Ernest smiles. "I'm glad. Go on."

"It was getting on, about midnight. I was sitting there feeling kinda high. But I wasn't. I mean, I wasn't on nothing. I was just, you know, trying to talk to God sorta. But I wasn't sure even there was a God. How can I know sitting there in the barrio rotting like everybody else? If there's a God, why doesn't he help me? I don't want to be in no ghetto. Mexico would be nice, maybe. My mother, she has people there, a brother."

"How were you feeling, sitting there in the church, Gabe?"

"Well, I was angry. At the end of my ropes. Like I could see the gang was going to ruin Sonny and maybe get us killed. Our Menudo is only like a dozen guys, from our neighborhood, not the famous one. We could be wiped out. Easy. I kinda feel like a father to Sonny, you know, even though he's just a couple years younger than me. While I was sittin' there, it started to rain. Seemed to me God was saying he cries for kids like Sonny, too. I got an idea then. And all this was going around in my head. Next thing you know, I was pounding the back of the pew in front of me and shouting something like, *If you're out there God, I want to know. I want to know tonight.*"

Gabriel's spontaneous reenactment resounds off the concrete walls and seems to startle him.

"Go on," Ernest encourages.

"I'd barely finished, like that, when I felt as if I'd been trapped inside a sunrise. Everything went completely white. I heard this crack over my head. Things began catching fire. I thought, 'This can't be happening. What's going on?' The church was a sandwich with fire in the middle. It was gradual, not like a bomb. In slow motion, like. I just sat there. And, finally, I realized 'I've gotta get outta here.' There was no way to save nothing. God had decided to burn this church. Out of everything in East L.A. that coulda been struck by lightning, the place I was sitting was struck. Nobody knew why. I didn't even realize why myself until I thought about it."

There isn't a breath drawn. Days of contrived responses from the Mexican-American chairman of the Standing Committee have been contrasted with the innocent impressions of one of the newest communicants in the diocese, so deftly, that Ernest Shriver's genius remains invisible to all but a few.

Bliss senses that Ernest planned this surprise for her benefit. She can work at this, calculating how to lay patchwork pieces of testimony atop the makeshift case the diocese has thrown together, or she can relax and let spontaneity continue to breathe life into the proceedings. Either way, she can trust her attorney to lead her through this valley of death.

"God," Gabriel isn't finished, "he sometimes talks in whirlwinds. Or in manna food that migrant peoples find on the ground to eat. But sometimes he burns a bush because one guy needs a lesson. Last year, I was the one guy. God, he would do that, for me. To get my attention. And the funny thing is, I didn't even know I was praying."

"What was your prayer, Gabriel?" Ernest asks.

"Just for my life to be better."

"Is it?"

"Well, yes. Sonny and me is no longer with Menudo. We got a new home with an English teacher and his sister from Ohio. I'm not saying God is going to burn down a church for every guy in a gang who wants out. But here's another thing. He won't have to get *my* attention that way again. Once you *know*, you know. Ya know? It's like I am proof now to other guys that one kid can leave Menudo, takin' another kid with him. I think that's the way it is with God. He sends one guy at a time to accomplish one thing. And why should Ascension want to help me so much when I'm the one started all their troubles?"

"Do you feel badly about that?"

"I don't blame myself for Sister's being on trial here, if that's what you mean. At first, I blamed myself for just sitting there so long, watching the place burn. But for the trouble since, I blame the gang that runs our church higher up. They don't know about one-to-one so much. You saw. None of them people who has the quarrel with Sister came here to explain why. Reverend Sparks isn't here. The bishop, he isn't here. At least, I don't think he is." Several onlookers chuckle. "I never seen the man myself."

Ernest jovially ad libs, "But you *have* met God."

"Once that I know of," Gabe answers.

"Mr. President," Ernest says, "I respectfully request that the testimony of this witness be highlighted in the copy of these proceedings that will be given to the prosecution's only witness, Mr. Hugh Comanito. I regret he chose not to stay and listen to any of the witnesses for the defense."

"I'm sorry, Mr. Shriver, it's not within our power to direct that transcripts be specially prepared for future readers."

No, Bliss realizes, *Ernest has to do that all by himself.*

* * *

"You've been charged," Averill Cunningham says to Bliss, as if she were a butterfly he'd pinned to styrofoam, "with willfully lying when you swore out a civil complaint against your bishop. Do you understand the charge?"

"Yes. And I understand that it hinges on knowing the legal meaning of a few terms, such as the term 'extinct,'" Bliss adds.

"Extinct," Cunningham repeats.

"I myself didn't know this term in its legal sense until I made inquiry." Bliss can feel herself switching from the spontaneous mode she used before the break to a more calculating one. *You gotta fight fire with fire,* she tells herself.

"What did you think extinct meant?" the Church Advocate asks.

"Before or after I had benefit of counsel?"

"Let's begin with before," Averill suggests.

"I thought it meant gone from the face of the earth, wiped out."

"That's the common understanding, is it not?"

"I believe so."

"So," Cunningham says, "when you swore that it was your bishop's intention to make Church of the Ascension extinct, you did *not* mean to say that he intended to wipe it from the face of the earth? You understood extinct in some *other* sense?"

"The bishop, wrongfully, though successfully, rendered my *parish* extinct in all senses of the word," Bliss says. She feels something akin to a Maypole in her spine. It feels as if dancers are securing footing in the pit of her stomach. Derek Hunter's gaze meets her eyes. He clenches a fist and shakes it. Bliss gets an adrenaline rush.

"You and your parishioners were in possession of a letter

from the bishop, were you not, in which he expressly stated his desire that Church of the Ascension continue its ministry in the East End?"

"We *are* in possession of one such letter, yes."

"And still, you went to the civil justice system accusing Bishop Charles Sprockett and layman Hugh Comanito of making your church extinct!"

"I registered a complaint. I indicated that my bishop's behavior led me to doubt the sincerity of his previous remarks. Our church is small, but we do well financially. The bishop had begun speaking about us as one does of congregations which are not self-sufficient. His fiduciary claim against our assets, causes our *parish* to be nonexistent, legally." Bliss takes a deep breath. She spots Sam near the back of the gallery. He blows a kiss. Another adrenaline rush.

Bliss continues. "In a most unchristian fashion, the diocese stripped us of financial control, removing, also, functioning clergy from our midst."

"Yourself."

"Yes. And even today, it is threatening to list our property for sale. This, when services have been conducted continuously on that site for longer than the Diocese of Los Angeles itself has existed."

Cunningham says coolly, "You sound hard done by. But don't diocesan bishops have the authority to step in when churches face extinction?"

"They do."

"Did not your own father face this situation on more than one occasion when he served as a diocesan bishop?"

"I'm certain he did, yes."

Ernest Shriver gets to his feet. "May I respectfully ask the court to remind the Church Advocate to refrain from making irrelevant references to the only member of the House of Bishops who has deigned to attend these proceedings, the Rt. Rev. Donald Birch, retired. And may I reiterate my previous request that the accused be allowed to face her accuser, the Rt. Rev. Charles Sprockett, directly; so that we can put an end to this compilation of hearsay evidence?"

"The record will reflect your concern," the President says.

18

Friendly Fire in a War of Words

November 20, 1991

//Conduct unbecoming a member of the clergy." Carolyn Banting is making oral notes on a tape recorder, reading from *The Findings of the Ecclesiastical Court* on her way to interviewing the judges. "Ms. Birch-Garland did violate her ordination vows. She shall not administer a church, preside at Eucharist, perform sacerdotal duties or participate in any Episcopal governing councils for twenty-four months. And we further stipulate that a violation of this suspension shall be grounds for another presentment."

Then Banting begins her own commentary. "When a handful of religious men condemn the perceived insolence of a spiritual woman, we can't feign shock. Today's judgment raises the specter of Joan of Arc and brings a best-selling novelist out of hiding to observe her misfortune firsthand. The defendant's attorney left no stone unturned, challenging a system that refused to make its case face to face. In the end, he also proved this reporter wrong. I've been saying there were no witnesses to the Ascension fire. But Shriver worked the peculiar magic which so often has brought him victory in Superior Court; he produced the only person who knows what happened the night Ascension burned."

Sam Garland has set up the press room for a post mortem conference. He greets everyone and thanks the justices for their participation. Only three of the five have come to be questioned and only four reporters and Derek Hunter are on hand to hear them. "Please identify yourselves," Sam says, nodding to Carolyn who has lifted her hand.

"Carolyn Banting, the *L.A. Times*. I'm surprised that you've cited the defendant for violating her ordination vow. Could you elaborate?"

"We aren't bound in the way a criminal jury would be," says the justice who was the "marble judge" in Bliss's pouch. "Since it's been obvious from the start that the defense intends to test our ruling, we feel the higher court deserves to receive the benefit of *all* our findings, especially those which may merit further investigation."

"Follow-up?" Carolyn looks to Sam and goes ahead. "You're saying it was appropriate to convict her of a crime you believe she committed even though she wasn't told to defend herself against it?"

The presiding justice takes over. "The majority of the members of the court have found Mrs. Birch, or the Reverend Birch-Garland as she is known in these ecclesiastical proceedings, guilty of 'conduct unbecoming a member of the clergy.' In identifying the forms of unacceptable conduct it feels she engaged in, the majority has pointed to something not itemized in the charges against her. Your observation is correct. And where today's judgment is over broad, a higher court can, of course, reverse it."

Derek Hunter cuts in without identifying himself, "Do you have any doubt they will?"

"They will have the opportunity, just as we had the opportunity to exonerate her, but didn't."

Sam reaches inside his jacket and pulls out two envelopes. "I have a statement here from my wife. The defendant, I should say. It's brief and, if I can get the right envelope, I'll read it to you. She says, 'While I've awaited the findings of this court, Anglican envoy Terry Waite has been released from captivity in Lebanon. Church people everywhere rejoice with him. And sadly, at the same time, L.A.'s own Magic Johnson has been taken hostage by the plague of our day, the HIV virus. In that light, my own tribulation comes into clearer perspective. I have my health, and I can continue to worship Almighty God when and wherever I choose, even as my job-action case against the Diocese of Los Angeles proceeds to another tribunal. I hope to be exonerated on appeal.'"

* * *

"Won't you stay for Thanksgiving?" Bliss asks her father when he announces after the verdict that he must be on his way.

"There's a little widow I've been seeing," he explains. "She wants to make me Thanksgiving dinner, any dinner really. I've been here long enough this time, Beebee. Peter White has spoken to me about returning in Lent and celebrating Easter with you. Perhaps I'll persuade Marie to come along. If you let me go."

"Of course, I'll let you go."

"You know, don't you, that I've never let go of you?" Donald says. "Even when I *didn't* support what you were doing . . ."

Bliss can only nod. She opens her arms and her father steps into them for a hug. Bliss is shocked to realize she is giving rather than receiving. She is the stronger. She is the one brimming over with deep affection as if she might be able to put all the unspoken gratitude of her life with him, into this one embrace.

"And I haven't let go of you," Bliss answers. "Don't be too long. It is much easier to hold the fort with you here than without you."

Donald steps back and looks Bliss in the eye. "That's what fortitude is for." He reaches gently to lift her chin. "Chin up. It won't be that long 'til we do this again. And with a better outcome, I think."

* * *

February 1992

The Rev. Elizabeth Sparks has no recourse but to draft a letter of resignation to the newly elected Standing Committee. Her fall from grace was swift. Although she put in countless hours of unpaid overtime editing the bishop's *Adharma* manuscript last summer, something she did very well, she wasn't able to get cooperation from Church of the Ascension. Her inability to keep Sprockett's name out of Carolyn Banting's feature articles has cost her dearly.

The axe had fallen six months ago. Returning from a proofreading weekend at the bishop's Catalina cabin, she found a notice on her desk advising that she look for work elsewhere and be gone by February. The same afternoon, the bishop came in for a heart-to-heart talk. He seemed to hint that something more personal might come of his and Elizabeth's relationship if she were to have no ties to his administration. Filled with this hope, Elizabeth continued serving Sprockett while she searched for secular employment in L.A. Without thinking it through, she cut herself off from the chance to make a timely transition, with the bishop's assistance, to another church position in a distant diocese.

Only after New Year's, as she saw herself falling off the official calendar, did Elizabeth face the challenge of reporting her experiences as Urban Deacon in the self-evaluation Charles Sprockett had asked her to file. Now she sees her situation all too clearly:

> From the beginning, I've been keenly aware that the players in this arena, the Diocese of Los Angeles, seem larger than life — more suited to grand opera. Neither the powers of reason, nor strategies of crisis intervention have been acceptable tools to the parties involved in the Ascension fire matter. What does this resemble? War.
>
> I myself was caught up in 'the cult of personality' around our bishop. His charms are hard to resist though Ascension's vestry apparently does not concur. They ignored directives from the chancellor as to their legal responsibility to the diocese. Now their priest bears the brunt of a discipline which rightfully, I think, belongs to us all. We backed away from the situation. Let proper penance be made. I suggest we tithe the notorious insurance money to a good cause anonymously. We have waged war over petty stakes pretending 'Tomorrow' was on the line. The future is on the line. But our battle, like its counterpart in the Gulf, did not resolve a single question that's important to human destiny.
>
> Church infighting diminishes us. Christian soldiers quietly embarrass themselves, but they draw only friendly fire. I myself have taken a shot. I'm bleeding. Of course getting wounded is inevitable. Those who work beside the big guns eventually stand in the wrong place at the wrong time. But, let me be clear. I do not regret my experiences. I'd serve here again in a minute, although I humbly submit my resignation.

Elizabeth puts a copy on Charles Sprockett's desk, hoping against hope he'll see himself more clearly in her evaluation. She imagines the situation can yet be turned around during this last week of her employment. The bishop has agreed to preside at staff Eucharist at 9:30 a.m. tomorrow, the day of her official retirement.

But morning comes and Sprockett is a no-show. In the afternoon, he stops by her office to offer an apology and to say that as soon as his divorce is final, he'll be announcing his engagement to a woman from the diocese of Rio Grande where he previously served. The future Mrs. Sprockett is a young woman he's known for years, though their friendship only blossomed when she chose him as the subject of her honors thesis at seminary.

"You know," Charles adds, "my ex is moving back to our old neighbourhood in Albuquerque, and will probably marry this fellow who was a tennis partner of mine. Our kids went to school together. It's a small world, isn't it?"

"Why did you ask me to stay in L.A.?" Elizabeth asks.

"If I suggested that, I'm sorry. I was at loose ends. When a lifelong relationship breaks down, you find yourself kind of whoring about for reassurance. If I seemed to encourage you, forgive me, Elizabeth. You made so many trips to the cabin. Maybe you read more into that than you should have. But I know I'm not the best at being clear about my feelings."

Elizabeth burns. "Is the chemistry between us to be explained away as a function of your inadequacy to be clear about your feelings?"

"I've always valued your analytical skills. And if that's how it seems to you, then that may well be the way it is. I like to think I do more good than harm, overall," Charles says.

"I like to think that, too. So, is this goodbye?" Elizabeth steps around from behind her desk to give him a hug.

He steps back. "Have they subpoenaed you?"

"What?"

"Does the National Board of Inquiry want to talk with you about your role in this Ascension business?"

"I haven't heard anything," Elizabeth says.

"Haven't we kept you up to speed? The Presiding Bishop himself is convening a panel now that the appeals briefs are on record. They want to establish whether or not I intimidated," he pauses as if to recall a name, "*anyone*. Even though you're leaving, we should have kept you apprised of this."

Elizabeth can't conceal her anger. She hits her fist against today's date on the calendar circled in red. "I didn't have any choice about leaving."

"That's right."

"Would you say I was *intimidated* into accepting the terms of severance I was offered?"

Charles doesn't avoid the confrontation. He's even gentlemanly as he presents what he considers *the facts* of Elizabeth's case. He takes a step closer, puts his left hand on the wall above their heads and leans toward her. "You were eased out. We could have prepared formal grounds for your dismissal. Not the least was your loose lip concerning my private life."

Elizabeth knows she spread the rumor of Charles' impending divorce before he'd told anyone else.

"As always," Charles says matter-of-factly, "you have been too thorough. I can't circulate the letter that you left on my desk. If you choose to mail it to anyone, that's your prerogative. However, in a month or two, you'll realize you've aired too much. If you want *me* to distribute something, have it on my desk before you leave." Charles withdraws his palm from its high perch, turns abruptly and is gone without a hug or a goodbye.

Tomorrow, I don't report to work here. Elizabeth feels like the guy in the commercial who is grateful for a slap in the face. The last six months have been nothing short of hell. The only bullet she dodged was running the media control room for the trial. She drew the line at that suggestion.

Elizabeth goes to Charles's office late in the day. She knows he's left for a confirmation service. She seats herself in his swivel chair, leans forward and helps herself to a sheet of the bishop's own letterhead. She borrows his pen and poises it above the page. Succumbing to the tactics of a theology of hostility which Sprockett has challenged time and again under various banners, Elizabeth scrawls a two-word version of her final thoughts:

"Up yours!"

19

Shake-ups and Shakedowns

"You are glowing," Sam says to Bliss. He comes in at 5:45 loaded with take-out food. He's insisted on keeping his nights to fix supper, even though Bliss has more time for such things since her inhibition.

"I've been," Bliss pauses, "visiting with *our* Sally."

Sam spreads the fare. "That takes my breath away."

It takes two hours for Bliss to recount her afternoon's experience though it lasted only minutes. "My reading habits are changing," she says. "Instead of a steady diet of magazine and newspaper pieces, I sometimes sit all afternoon, like today, with a Madeleine L'Engle book. Then, at one point, I looked up from it. I saw a ray of sunlight that had broken in through the glass curtains. It began collecting itself in one place on the coffee table and was growing there until, I swear, it looked like a host—the priest's own. I realized, for me, it's getting harder to . . . let go of being the one. The one who raises up the body of Christ."

"I know," Sam consoles. He takes Bliss's hand and says a short blessing over their meal, giving thanks, as well, for Bliss's day.

"I saw a bright image in my mind of the light streaming from the host raised in Communion. It's a thought I haven't had before, that the host is a sun in that moment. We tend to think of the sun as an energy source. But really, it's the Source acting through the sun. Standing behind it, even as the priest stands behind the raised host. Then the light on the table literally broke apart. It was free. It tumbled and it flew. I can't describe what I saw. It was so impossible I finally closed my eyes. That's when I remembered I'd seen light behave in this odd way once before.

"I'd been walking on a trail near our campsite, without you, when I surprised a small fox. It seemed frozen in place ahead of me in a patch of sunlight. The little fellow looked me in the eye, in a most arresting way, as if to say, 'Stop and *experience* this.' So I did. The fox darted into the underbrush. But he seemed to take me and some of the light with him. I felt an invigorating connection with Fox and with Sun. I stepped onto the spot where the little animal had been and felt electricity charge up my spine until it exploded, like a fireball, in my head. Did I mention it at the time?"

"I don't think so," Sam says.

"I'm sure I had no words for it. It was simultaneously personal and cosmic—as if the fuel of a thousand stars had joined the juices that power Me and Fox and Sun.

"When I opened my eyes after remembering that experience, flecks of crystal were literally dancing around our living room. I could feel the same excitement I'd felt in the forest years ago. It was making me warm. I had to stand up and dance with it. Then, a sunbeam looked me in the eye and said, 'Mother?' It sang to me, 'Over here. See?' A glistening particle fell back onto the table exactly where the holy wafer had been. I sat back down, and particle by particle all the dancing light reassembled itself there. Then it rose like a morning mist in front of my face."

Bliss is into a second helping of cashew chicken and Sam, though finished, doesn't begin cleaning up.

"And this mist asked me, I know this sounds strange . . ."

"It's okay, 'inquiring minds want to know,'" Sam encourages.

"That's it. Exactly." Bliss chuckles at the timing of Sam's *National Inquirer* aside. "It asked, 'Is there anything you'd like to know?' It wasn't an audible question, just something I sensed. I didn't consciously reply. But as it continued, I sensed it was really our Sally speaking. She told me, 'I stay at grandmother's side. She hasn't awakened to her powers. I simply surround her with love, with *your* love, mama.' She quoted, 'We shall not all sleep, but we shall all be changed' and asked whether I understood her. That's when I heard myself calling, 'Sally?' Out loud.

"And she answered. This is the part I want to remember, she said, 'It's hard for memories to heal when one isn't upheld in memory.'"

Sam repeats the sentence and asks what it means.

"My mother isn't yet into her power the way Sally is. She doesn't remember me the way Jim Pike remembers you."

Sam considers. "I suppose there *is* a function of memory attached to our communication."

"The misty light came closer and closer. I finally shut my eyes it was so bright. That's when I heard Sally say, 'I'm part of your halo, the protection surrounding one in whom all energies unite.' She promised she would guide my dreaming . . . and show me . . .'" Bliss is overcome, recalling something she'd forgotten.

Sam reaches for both of his wife's hands.

"This is so beautiful. I'd almost forgotten," Bliss goes on, "she said, 'Daddy has some friends here.' Even though my eyes were shut, she used the light. And I could see it, forming luminous letters. The letters of her name." Bliss traces S, A, L, L and Y in capitals in front of Sam's eyes, "Like to be *sure* I knew."

"Wait right there," Sam says. "I want to read you something those friends of mine said to me this morning." He clears away the empty plates as he gets up, and returns with his notebook. "They made an acrostic out of the word 'going,' to explain what they meant by feet, a discipline they want fire walkers to know." He shows her:

G = *Get an impression of where to go and, using your better instincts, go.*

O = *Only by evaluating your travels will you learn to obey orders.*

I = *Improve your means of travel as you can. Why go by ark where arc is available?*

N = *Never go alone. Take counsel with those who've gone before.*

G = *Go inward, accepting the aid of the saints appointed to direct your going.*

Affirm, "I'm in the right place to coincide with what I need to experience." You are never alone. Whenever one opens to the Christed Self, protection is in place. Come to the Place of Abiding, where angelic oversight is abundant.

The phone rings. It's Ernest Shriver, and Bliss puts him on the speaker phone.

"Great news. They've set the date for your appeal. Monday, the sixth of July. The venue, this will tickle you, Sam, is Grace Cathedral, San Francisco. One of the lay members appointed to the court is a retired justice of the Ninth District Circuit Court of Appeals. Cunning Ham is going to be skewered."

Ernest takes a little more pleasure in this conclusion than Bliss feels comfortable hearing.

"So," she asks, "will their findings be announced by September?" She's considering when she might resume her priestly duties, when the fence around The Pit can come down and rebuilding begun.

"Well, no. We're looking at six months, or more. Birthing a written decision is like a pregnancy. Six to nine months, I'm afraid. In all likelihood, your suspension will be lifted by the court just weeks before it runs out of its own accord. You know, in the legal world, two years is a drop in the bucket."

"Small victory," Sam says.

"It will be big enough when we regain control of Ascension's monies. And Bliss, I have good news on that score. The firm is returning half the retainer your people advanced me. Defending your honor hasn't been that costly. How many did you have in church last Sunday?"

"Thirty-eight."

"You're gonna make it. That's great. We could see all the way to the foothills from our place Sunday, and I felt it was a sign everything is clearing up. Have a good evening, you two."

Sam speculates at once as to whether the Giants will be playing at home in early July. "I haven't seen Candlestick since the quake," he says.

"You haven't seen Grace Cathedral since then either," Bliss reminds him. It's where they were married, and Bliss has always regarded the stately edifice and its beautiful front doors fondly. It was on a Monday in May, twenty-six years ago. There was no organ music. No soloist to mark the occasion. Bliss didn't walk down the aisle on her father's arm wearing a satin dress with a train. Rather, she showed up in the bishop's office wearing a white wool suit. Still . . .

"You know, I could go the rest of my life without seeing that place again," Sam says almost sleepily. "It's too sad. That's where Jim Pike was mortally wounded."

"I thought you were dreaming of becoming a bishop there?" Bliss hears herself sigh.

"I may have said as much, a long time ago. I imagined, then, that the way to be lord of your affections was to take charge of a diocese. Grand Pooh Bah, just like your daddy. But, anymore, the idea . . ." It is rare for Sam Garland to drop his thoughts mid-sentence.

"If Jim Pike could come back tomorrow," Bliss speculates, "do you think he'd reincarnate as a Christian?"

"Would Jesus Christ?"

"I'm serious."

"Well, I have no clue," Sam says. "What about yourself? Would you be a Christian in another life, Beeb?"

Bliss doesn't answer that. "We were *both* students of the Socratic method sometime back, weren't we?"

"Don't bother your head with too many met afores," Sam suggests, breaking the word *metaphor* the way Ernest Shriver divides *Cunningham*. "You want your job back. So keep on track." The automatic advice has the ring of a rap lyric. "Ready for bed?" He offers his hand.

Bliss doesn't ask Sam if he can feel the breeze at their backs as they climb the outside stairs. She said yes to an early bedtime; there's no more to say. The breeze is a poet's wind. The first rush of the wind of the next millennium. And it's blowing through her. It sings about the long journey: *You aren't alone anymore.* Liberty and justice "once and for all" are for all. Sam, so recently broken back on himself when his longings, long suppressed, came to the fore, is being born again.

There was a moment there moments ago, when he accepted the challenge of helping her put her blinders on. After an enlightening afternoon you can't keep glowing, you must get going. Even this interlacing of fingers is scarcely necessary, Bliss knows.

* * *

Monday, June 29, 1992

"I can still think on my feet," Sam brags. Andrea Marvin has asked the question of the day, "Where were you when the quakes came?"

"I looked into the startled faces of my 8 o'clockers as we waited out that second one. With no sense of panic, I joked, 'Looks as if we're going to perform a rock mass this morning. Take shelter under the pews if it's necessary.' It was dueling disaster stories after the service. Bliss and I weren't here in '71, but everyone who *was*, assured us this wasn't anything like the jolt back then."

Andrea agrees. "Mom says '71 was more terrifying—like you

were on a bucking bronco. No matter how it jerked, you couldn't be bucked off. She says in '71 there was a sense of dread, fear of an impending disaster. This reminded her of a freight train going by. It would pass."

Sam picks up the idea that earthquake stories cross generational lines. "Bliss's parents were so impressed by news of a disastrous earthquake that struck in India on their wedding day, a year later they used the name of the province where it struck— Bihar— as her middle name."

"'Landers.' It was probably somebody's name to begin with."

* * *

Monday, July 6, 1992

"It's hard to walk away without knowing the verdict. I'm afraid, Sam. Afraid to hope for it."

"Shriver was brilliant today, Beeb. There's no doubt whatever you're going to win." Sam reaches to pick up the newspaper the stewardess gave them. He points to Carolyn Banting's name in a shared byline. "It's amazing. Your woman can find us even at 27,000 feet. I don't think she's made it onto the front page before."

"Already?" Bliss assumes the piece must be about her appeal.

"She's found somebody who earns his living translating channeled material into Japanese. Apparently the Asians are very eager for that." Sam hands over the section.

The decision to fly home this evening instead of spending another night in San Francisco was made by a nervous secretary in the law offices of Thornburg, Shriver and Armacost about noon. Continuing aftershocks, taken with the news that a tropical storm is expected to inundate L.A. with rain—something unknown in summer—persuaded the woman to make new arrangements. There was a limo waiting at the cathedral when the hearing concluded at 4:30. They had only ten minutes at the hotel to pack. Sam had to phone his favorite Russian restaurant and renege on reservations for twelve, practically half the house.

"I'll miss the borscht," Bliss says, "but the idea of sleeping in my own bed sounds good. Providing we aren't turned back by hurricane-force winds." She lays the paper aside. "Imagine. If the Japanese are lapping up Shirley MacLaine, think what Pike's thoughts might mean to them."

"It will all be dismissed." Sam's tone is dismissive. "MacLaine says one of the sources for *Out on a Limb* was communicating to her from a station in outer space, for heaven's sake."

"I'm just thinking that those notebooks of yours don't have legs. If Pike's message could speak to Japan, you're the one who'd have to hand it over for translation."

Sam digs for his wallet. He pulls out two small note cards. "Ideas are in the air," he says. "In the west, we're consumed with turning them into property. Imagine telling the world you've patented the process of getting a second wind. No one can experience getting a second wind anymore without giving you credit, without paying a royalty. Here," Sam hands Bliss the cards, "from *Adharma*. Sprockett—I give him credit—is determined to pull ideas out of the air to help his readers compare their way of doing things with a completely different way. He's giving Eastern thought a shape we in the West may be able to tolerate."

> The story is told of the computer scientist and the Taoist shop owner who went for a walk together. "Aren't the birds joyful this morning?" the Taoist commented.
> "You're not a bird, so you can't know they're joyful," the scientist responded.
> "Well, my learned friend, you're not me, " the Taoist answered. "So you can't know for sure that I don't know how to perceive how happy these birds are."

> Christians, by and large, don't perceive relative situations and complementary opposites the way Zen Buddhists and Taoists do. The Occidentalist prefers to render judgment. The Orientalist often adopts a wait-and-see attitude.

"You've always been good at going with the flow, Sam," Bliss says. "Very Eastern. You've already made the midlife transition I'm struggling with."

"What's that?"

"You know how to be a point of light."

"And you don't?"

"I'm still in mourning," she lifts an imaginary host, "having been moved away from the sun."

* * *

Wednesday, October 14, 1992

"So, nothing is missing?" the policeman asks.
"Nothing but the suspect ," Charles Sprockett answers. He's filing an assault complaint against an absent, unnamed assailant.
"I mean, no stolen property." The officer sounds as if it's an effort for him to be patient.
The clerk inside saw nothing that happened outside. That's what he says. Charles isn't certain it's true. But for the purposes of the police report, the bishop can't argue the point. There's no missing property, although there would have been if Charles hadn't taken matters into his own hands after the thief ripped the video bag from his grasp.

* * *

Thursday, November 5, 1992

Bill Clinton and Al Gore are victorious. So is Takahanada, a young wrestler who took Charles' fancy in person when he attended the Grand Sumo Tournament in Tokyo in September. Taka (whose brother Waka, is also a wrestler) picked up his second tournament victory in the recent Aki Basho. Charles Sprockett's bruises have faded and he's ready to write about his attack for his monthly column:

> *Is a binge or purge orgy more in order when the Grand Old Party fails to retain its hold on the U.S. Presidency? At any rate, I've decided to purge. I do confess, I'm a violent man.*
>
> *When provoked by a teenager a few weeks ago, I engaged him in a knock-down, drag-out fight and, yes, I enjoyed the accompanying adrenaline rush. As someone who's never been high on drugs or alcohol, I now know how seductive the stimulant called hand-to-hand combat can be. During our engagement, I felt as young as my opponent.*
>
> *I'd ducked out on the National League championship game to drive to a convenience store for a video. Not any corner market. And not your ordinary video. This was the only outlet in the city my secretary, Blanche Peters, could locate that carries the digest of each Ozumo (Grand Sumo) tournament from Japan. I've developed more than a passing interest in the ancient sport*

cherished in the Land of the Rising Sun. Nowhere have I found a sporting medium that integrates flesh and spirit as well as sumo does for the Japanese.

Since I'd witnessed only a single evening performance in person, I was anxious to lay my hands on the summary of all fifteen nights of competition. Having determined (wrongly) that Pittsburgh was, indeed, to provide the U.S. home team for the first international World Series, my thoughts turned to seeing how things had come out at the Aki Basho, Tokyo's "fall classic."

I'd been in possession of the long-desired sumo tape less than a minute and was returning to my car outside the Little Tokyo convenience store, when a young Latino snatched my wallet and the sack containing the video digest. Except for my driver's license and a credit card, the wallet was practically empty. I didn't give any thought to the ten or twenty dollars that might still be in it. Without that bag, I might never witness the outcome of the basho.

I lit out after the suspect shouting, "Keep the wallet, but drop that bag." I said it several times. Then I tried the same thing in Spanish, though not very well.

My valuing the video more than my wallet triggered some curiosity on the thief's part. The young man shortened his stride and I was able to cover the distance between us as he seemed to puzzle over my request. But as I got close, he turned on me.

"You religious?" he asked, staring at my clerical collar. He jiggled the bag. "You gonna watch a dirty movie tonight?" Perversion was the only explanation of my behavior plausible to him. It suited him to stereotype me, just as I, admittedly, was seeing him as a hoodlum. I certainly hadn't imagined engaging him in a conversation. His tone of voice indicated he'd made a final judgment.

When he turned and ran again, I continued to give chase. Finally, I lunged at him and grabbed him around the waist. I can replay our fall in slow motion. I'd pinned his arms. His face was going to make contact with the concrete even as mine was protected. His cry was like a sharp bark as I fell on him.

"Give me the bag. Just give me the bag." I was panting. And I remember adding, "I want what belongs to me."

"You'll get yours," is what the boy growled back. I didn't like the look in his eye. I saw his foot out of the corner

of my eye. Then it was in my face. Strange as it sounds, I was invigorated by the blow. Before I realized it, I'd pulled us both to our feet and had relieved the youngster of my wallet. Only the video remained a point of contention. I was well into a long explanation of why I didn't want to be robbed, when the young man dropped the bag and loped off into the night with something about my being a strange bastard on his lips.

I'd won. But it seemed in that moment that I'd lost. I considered following the boy, though I knew better. The only thing I'd been robbed of was a chance to get off a clean punch. And, for some reason, that was on my mind. Who he was and why he was hanging around this parking lot didn't seem to concern me. The sumo tape was my consolation prize for not having gotten the chance to test my ability to avenge myself.

Why do I confess?

People who see my weekend side don't think much about my weekday face. Or I might say, my weak day-to-day face. If we are to find strength in weakness, learning to become conscious of each motivation is important. My administration is known for its proactive rather than reactive management style. Having tasted reaction so up close and personal, while the Phillies were making their comeback as the Jays' opponent, I'm glad the leaders of great societies keep prompting us to stop venting anger through violence. For as God's reign comes, the Peaceable Kingdom of the Holy is restored to lowly flesh and blood. Lamb and lion (strange roaring bastards that we are), must study war no more. Little by little, we understand better, how to claim, "The battle belongs to the Lord."

20

After a Full Three Hundred Sixty

Sunday, January 17, 1993

*B*lanche Peters is spellbound. Sam Garland is preaching the sermon of his life, the best she's heard from him in fourteen years. Instead of using his prepared text, he's speaking without it. But that isn't the only thing. The message imparts a deep, profound hope.

"Jesus was *always* in a state of epiphany, unashamed of showing forth Sophia. The host of heaven and the angels of our planet, await a rebirth of Wisdom, the wonder that's been promised in Christ, to the children of the next millennium, a new generation."

Blanche is sitting in her usual pew in the middle section, two people from the end, near the left-side aisle. But Sam Garland is not in his usual spot. Freed from the prepared pages he usually follows, he's been moving about. If anything, he's less at ease, but more energized than usual. He looks feisty. And feisty isn't a word Blanche would have associated with her rector. He's too handsome for feisty, and too tall.

It seems, that without the text drawing him back, Sam is extending himself to people in the congregation, one after another. "When an individual surrenders to the All in all," he says, "Christ returns, bestowing the blessing of life eternal in just the way it has always been given, to one heart at a time."

The words "one heart" set Blanche's mind spinning. She takes a few deep breaths and looks around the church. One by one she encounters the saints portrayed in the stained glass windows— the apostles, the women, the Lord of all. She recalls the words of a British patriotic hymn, "I Vow To Thee My Country," that her mother learned as a child in England. The old woman has been singing "and soul by soul and silently, her shining bounds increase" to Blanche off and on ever since the wedding of Charles and Diana where she heard it sung again.

Blanche is caught up in reverie. The boundaries of her heart seem to be expanding with her inner vision. She sees people, not in All Souls' windows of glass but in her mind. They're robed in white. Walking in pairs along a bright path, they carry in their arms the blossoming flowers of desert, mountain and island. As she looks ahead at the sea of people, Blanche enjoys the carpet of flowers. It's a moving, magical carpet. Blanche supposes this caravan is moving toward the gates of heaven. She hovers above the scene, watching. Then, it becomes clear. These are angels. Their backs turned to the gates of heaven, they advance to greet the recently departed one by one. This welcoming party is a contingent of The Blessed. Blanche sees 72,000 pairs of angels—the 144,000.

Blanche sees herself reaching out to one of them, asking, "Do you have my invitation to the eternal homecoming?"

Then, a voice. For no reason she can fathom, Blanche knows she's heard it before. The quality of its tenor is as distinctive as James Earl Jones's bass, the assurance as familiar as Walter Cronkite's. It is the voice of Jesus, and Blanche realizes she didn't expect to hear it, here on earth, again.

* * *

Monday, January 18, 1993

"Today's lessons remind us that the mystery of human origin is held in God's knowledge of us before our earthly births. When the prophet Isaiah saw his people losing touch with their genealogical history, he preached, as I do."

Sam turns off the tape recorder. "I don't remember saying any of this," he tells Andrea. "I've listened to it three times since yesterday, and I still have no idea what prompted me to lay aside my notes and preach about the Second Epiphany. That isn't even the way we say it. We just say Epiphany."

"So, what happened?" Andrea asks.

"I sort of went into a trance. And Bishop Pike, maybe, or one of his cohorts in the spirit world, one of The Seventy, came along and managed to preach a pretty good sermon, through me."

"What did it feel like?"

"Like I woke up from a dream at the end of *my* sermon. There was a feeling of, I'd call it pleasant surprise, in the congregation. And acceptance. I hadn't noticed 'til then, but there was a smoggy haze hanging above their heads. Definitely blue. And for a little while after, I felt as if my legs were stronger, more muscular, than they actually are. Am I making sense?"

"Go on."

"While it was happening, I felt as if with each breath I drew, I was bringing more air into my lungs than I usually do, or better air. I was dying to have the service conclude so I could sit down and really listen to what I was saying. Because—how can I explain this? I had to, well, tend to the details of things like keeping my eyes open and my mouth lubricated. It felt as if I were the projectionist. The film couldn't run without me, but I had nothing to do with what was *on* the film."

"Did you get any unusual feedback?"

"Retired Bishop Ulricksen, who drops in maybe once a month, pumped my hand and said, 'Son, I declare you sound more like Jim Pike all the time.' He's *never* said anything before about my reminding him of Pike. I wouldn't have supposed the comparison very likely."

"Was it Ulricksen, then, who put the idea in your mind that it *was* Pike coming through?" Andrea asks.

"Oh, no. I had that impression when I felt it coming on."

"You felt it coming?"

"There were several lines in the Psalm. 'I desire to do your will,' was one. 'He has put a new song in my mouth,' was another. When I heard them, I had a sense that I was being asked to accept an invitation long ago engraved. Understand?"

"Not really. You feel the scripture itself, the Psalm, planted the idea in your mind that you should lay aside your notes?"

"Something like that. I knew, from years of opening my journal, that I was able to hear. What I didn't understand until just minutes before I was to preach, was the purpose of all that dutiful, daily listening. I've been in training for twenty-five years, preparing to speak this way. To speak when spoken to, you might say."

Andrea can't fully absorb Sam's answer. He's the only person in her experience who hears voices without them making him sick. "Would you be able to preach this way again?" She doesn't wait for an answer. "You know how it goes with us more scientific types. We need to replicate every experiment. One shot deals are no better than an extra-marital affair, nothing to write home about."

Sam and Andrea have already devoted time in several sessions to talking out the reasons for their brief dip into the shimmering pool of passion. There were several childhood insecurities that returned to threaten the secure footing Sam had attained in adulthood. Still, Andrea's sensuality is ever present to him. Sam has to shake it off again before he can answer her.

"If I felt the invitation in the same persuasive way again, I think I could let go. It was very compelling, almost like I didn't have any business giving it a second thought. That was the hardest part, not knowing what was happening, really; and wondering if I was, if *they* were, just making a spectacle of me."

"So, after listening, you approve of what was said?"

Sam lifts a finger. "Interesting point. Some of it is pretty strange. At the time, maybe people only picked up on the fact that my *way* of preaching was different. He's not tied to his notes this morning? Interesting. Those who said anything were very positive about that. But, here's the thing. A lot of people who don't usually sign up to receive a copy of the sermon by mail, signed up. I think, like me, they realize they want to delve into this message at their leisure."

"And are you concerned that you may be hung out to dry if this New Age method comes to light?"

"What makes you say New Age?" Sam squirms.

"You don't think so?"

"It's as old as the hills. Charismatics have their version. Why, some of the most respected literature of the early church, though it wasn't included in the Bible, came about this way. What's been happening to me in meditation over the years is like what happened to a fellow named Hermas. He was a brother of the Bishop of Rome. Not so different from my being essentially adopted by the Bishop of California. Hermas communed regularly with an angel and wrote down what he heard. Historians believe the messages from Hermas' shepherd, that's what he called his angel, were read aloud in churches. The commands and similes he received proved to be of tremendous value to people seeking spiritual direction. With candidates for baptism, his texts were used like scripture. But they aren't in our Bible. Too New Age, I guess."

"Can this be the first time I've said 'New Age' to you?"

Andrea's face is animated. "I had no idea you could be this defensive."

Sam winces. "So much has been dumped on the phrase. I wouldn't want it to taint the clarity," Sam pauses, "of the Second Epiphany. Or, its angels. There's baggage attached to that label."

"So you are ready," Andrea says. "You will replicate this occasion," she gestures toward the tape recorder Sam brought.

Sam catches her sense of anticipation. "What if, for the Church's sake, the energy that was once, say, John Donne, could come forward and update one of his remarkable messages? Or, imagine a Billy Graham or a Robert Schuler anticipating having a future opportunity to frame the faith again for novitiates?"

"It would be Schuler's kind I'd worry about crucifying you. I'm sorry, but you can't persuade me TV evangelists' concerns are primarily spiritual," Andrea says. "Their messages about success simply encourage and promote materialism."

Sam would like to take Andrea's hand, but he doesn't. "I think you've let yourself get trapped stereotyping fundamentalists," he says. "You see them as hypocrites. Easy enough to do. But my experience suggests the very power they preach about can turn them around. After a full three-sixty, their heads are screwed on better. But all you'll notice, at first, is that they're heading in the same direction as before."

Andrea is laughing. "What an optimist you are!" She tips her head up to the ceiling, leaning back in her chair.

* * *

Tuesday, January 19, 1993

Bishop Sprockett tosses a cassette onto Blanche Peters' desk when he comes in at 9:45 a.m. She hands him the paper and opens her supply drawer to peel a label she's already typed for this tape. Normally, Blanche sticks the appropriate label on the bishop's Sunday tape and files the cassette immediately in an archive box in the storage room. It takes thirty seconds.

"You're gonna have to transcribe this one, Blanche," Charles says. "I've had some requests for printed copies. Make ten for me and get a couple dozen over to St. James, by the weekend. Go ahead and put a copy of it in Linda's box, too. She may be able to get my next column from it."

"Right." Blanche is used to having to incorporate things into her schedule that aren't part of her routine. It seems best, this morning, to get this transcription out of the way immediately. The office will be bustling the hour before lunch with volunteers coming to collate a women's guild mailing.

After fast forwarding to the sermon, Blanche starts taking notes in shorthand. After five minutes, she stops the tape and places a call to Francine Goodwin, the secretary at All Souls. "I'm wondering if you've typed up Father Garland's sermon from Sunday," she asks. "Great. Could you fax me a copy?"

Francine has a question for Blanche. "Has news of Sam's sermon reached the bishop already?"

"I don't think so. Why?"

"I put it in the mail to you yesterday, but I can fax it, sure. You know, nearly fifty people signed the roster this week. Along with the shut-in and snowbird lists, that makes over two hundred copies. I wish I'd been on hand to hear it. Was it as inspired as it looks?" Francine isn't an Episcopalian. Like many larger churches, All Souls' employs grounds and office staff from outside the parish to avoid the appearance of playing favorites.

"It was different," Blanche confirms. "I was transported into my own thoughts. Missed a great deal of it, actually."

"So that's why *you* want a copy," Francine adds.

That isn't why Blanche needs a copy, but she isn't ready to explain this to Francine.

* * *

With Sam Garland's sermon in hand, Blanche now listens to the rest of Bishop Sprockett's Sunday message without trying to get it down. What she needs to do, she realizes as she follows along, is compose herself:

> *God's universal compassion—as embodied in Jesus, in Buddha, in Mithra and many others—is also, if we will admit it, asking to be embodied in us. Instead of making admissions of guilt, we need to make admissions of love. The components of this universal compassion are identified by the Apostle Paul in the confession he taught his Corinthian converts. To each member, he gave a motif. He advised the newest members of the House of Israel, almost as if by tribe, on fourteen points:*
> *1) Do everything in love.*

2) Build well.
3) Judge nothing before its appointed time.
4) Be generous.
5) Married or single, give your undivided attention to God.
6) Seek the good of others.
7) Forsake bad company.
8) Fix your eyes on the Unseen.
9) Be the prophet who doesn't peddle the Word for profit.
10) Aim for perfection.
11) Live in peace.
12) Have the mind of Christ in you.
13) Get a second opinion.
14) Run the race of Life expecting victory, and the crown of Eternal Light, the victor's wreath, will be yours.

Corinth lost sight of the way to honor Creation. But we've forgotten her corruption. The legacy of the faith given to Christians there outshines their unfaithfulness. Paul's words become a blueprint for leaving the degradation of urban, or urbane, existence. His converts are to be the leaven in the loaf. The epistle brings fresh instruction even now, at the close of the second millennium. We are the remnant. We await a glorious Second Epiphany. And in the days ahead, we'll live to see Moses' prayer answered: all Yahweh's children will become prophetic. The world awaits the edification of her prophets.

May you who have received this message prepare your hearts to sing as the psalmist did, 'There's a new song in my mouth: O, that today, we would harden not our hearts as our forebearers did, in the wilderness.' Amen.

As Blanche suspected, the text of her rector's sermon and the tape of Sprockett's message are identical. She gets up and enters the bishop's office silently, announced only by a gentle rap on the door. She takes a seat and waits for Charles' attention. Blanche appears composed, but inside she is in a dither. She's given no thought to what she's going to say.

"Yes. What is it, Blanche?"

"Is there a sermon preparation service both you and Father Garland subscribe to?" She shakes the pieces of paper in her hand, then stands and leans across the bishop's desk to put the faxed sermon in front of him. "This is the sermon I heard Sam Garland preach Sunday. Francine faxed it over. I haven't typed yours yet."

"Of course." Charles pauses. He's looking Blanche in the eye and she shifts her gaze back to the papers. "Oh. I should read it?" "It's identical to your tape. I was there. I heard Father Garland preach it. Now, I hear it from you on the tape. They made it on Sunday?"

"Yes. The second Sunday of Epiphany. Cycle A. But, it was just a spontaneous decision on my part to speak impromptu." Charles seems perplexed, and Blanche suspects he's imagining that *she's* dropped a stitch.

She takes a deep breath. "What's going on?" The words come out barely above a whisper.

Bishop Sprockett leans back. Then he takes up the fax and begins reading it in earnest. About halfway through, he picks up and dials his new wife's private number. With his free arm, he signals that he wants Blanche to stay put. "You must have prayed a powerful prayer somewhere along the line, Blanche Peters," he says while waiting for his wife to pick up. "You're the witness. The first. The Mary Magdalene on Easter morning, that's you."

Sandy Morgan, the new Mrs. Sprockett, is a part-time religion instructor at the University of Southern California. At her request, she and Charles have rented an apartment close to the campus. It houses a good part of their private libraries and serves as an in-town getaway for them. No one, other than Blanche, knows the phone number there.

Blanche isn't used to hearing the bishop say her last name. Just hearing him say, "Peters," somehow moves them closer to the core of this mystery.

The bishop leans forward. "Sandy, hi Hon. There's a book of mine, I don't know if it's been unpacked or not. I'd like to find it. It's called, I think, *Agrapha: The Non-canonical Writings of the Early Church*, but maybe only *The New Testament Apocrypha*. I need it. The cover may be red. If you can locate it without too much trouble, would you call me back? But don't mess up your schedule. It isn't lower case life and death, just the big kind. Love you."

Turning to Blanche, Charles says, "Well, I think we better ask your rector to come in."

"And tell him what?"

"That I have a tape I want him to hear."

Blanche puts both hands on the edge of Charles' desk. "It was a bigger wind than usual, the one blowing in from the sea this

Sunday," she says.

Charles smiles. "There are times I believe you know everything that's going on in this diocese, Blanche-who-ponders-it-all. Is it true they drew lots for the Sundays of '93, shooting for the time I'd make no nautical reference? Will the winner collect? I don't think there's anything about seafaring in that sermon. *This* sermon," he adds, tapping Sam's.

Blanche decides she can answer without breaking a confidence. "You do have 104 active clergy," she says, "and that divides quite nicely by 52. Multiplied by ten, it's a handsome sum. You'll have to put thumb screws to the dean of the Cathedral if you want to know who's dividing the $1040 purportedly at stake." Changing her tone, Blanche asks, "How did it happen?"

"The sermon?"

"Something prompted you both to depart from your prepared remarks. What was it?" Blanche asks.

"I just felt, well, that Paul's message is simpler than we think. It's not like I haven't preached off the cuff before. I didn't give it any thought. I was pulling thoughts out of thin air, so to speak. I never imagined anyone else could, you know, breathe that same air. Get wind of the *very* same thing?"

"It's the wind of the next millennium," Blanche says. She's given her observation no thought. It comes . . . out of nowhere.

"The wind of the next millennium," Charles repeats. "Yes."

* * *

Sam Garland's delay in making an appearance at diocesan head-quarters Tuesday afternoon isn't deliberate. Instead of arriving at 1:30, as he'd supposed he could, it's almost 2:30. Blanche shows him into Bishop Sprockett's office. As she excuses herself, the bishop says, "Would you put the tape of my Sunday sermon on, over the intercom, Blanche? I'll control the volume."

Charles indicates a seat for Sam.

"I understand your sermon on Sunday came as a spontaneous offering. Blanche says there was an element of mystery about it."

"Francine told me you'd requested a copy."

"Blanche asked for it. She made a puzzling discovery when she went to transcribe *my* message. I also preached off the cuff on Sunday and, it appears, tapped into the same source you did. The identical source, in fact." The bishop turns up the volume on his intercom. Sam's eyes flash with recognition. This is a sermon he knows by heart just two days after preaching it.

The bishop hands Sam a book. "I had my wife drop this off," Sprockett says. The tape continues to play. "Take a look at Chapter 21 of *Nicodemus.*"

Sam caresses the black-bound volume. It is embossed with gold lettering, *Lost Books of the Bible*. Opening it, he notices that this edition was published in Newfoundland. It bears a 1926 copyright. Although he's seen various collections of works which early church councils declined to include in the Bible, Sam hasn't seen this particular one. The chapter Bishop Sprockett has pointed out tells the afterlife story of the sons of Simeon. Two of them are numbered among five hundred souls said to have come out of their graves at the time of Jesus' resurrection.

Charinus and Lenthius arose, but they remained mute. Unable to speak, they told their stories by writing them down in front of witnesses. Neither knew what the other was writing, until it was revealed that their messages duplicated each other to the letter. Charinus' work was witnessed by Annas, Caiaphas and Gamaliel while Nicodemus and Joseph watched Lenthius write. No sooner had the brothers made their simultaneous witness than they were translated once again to those realms from which they had so briefly returned.

"What do you make of it?" Charles asks, turning the intercom off.

Sam considers. "Simultaneity isn't unknown. There's Pentecost. But apparently *this* account was considered too fanciful. Sounds more like a magician's trick than a work of the Spirit."

Charles reaches for the book. "What I mean is, what do you make of its having happened, to *us* ?"

"I haven't had time to ponder that. But, I can tell you, I've done nothing since Sunday except think about what its having happened to *me* means. I don't want members of my congregation saying I channeled a sermon, even though that *is*, essentially, what happened."

Charles leans forward. "You know the source?"

"None other than the Rt. Reverend James A. Pike, deceased. He's been my spiritual director and mentor for the last thirty-seven years."

Charles swallows hard. "You're sure?"

Sam tries to retrieve something appropriate to the occasion from his store of pithy sayings. "It was Oscar Wilde, wasn't it, who said that mysteries in this world are of the invisible rather than the visible variety? What we've experienced *is* a mystery. Of the audible rather than the inaudible variety," Sam says. "I admit, I'm the one who told my counselor, months ago, that I'd feel better if my messages from Pike came through more people than just me. If that was a prayer, then, I guess, you're the answer."

"The uninitiated would assume nothing could stand in the way, now, of our developing a friendship."

"We know something more about one another, yes. But knowledge is powerless," Sam observes. "It can't make pain disappear. Just because we've danced this dance, I can't assure Bliss everything is going to be all right. And what's even harder, for me, I've discovered that I'm a very reluctant medium."

Charles gets up. He carries the book of lost epistles over to his bookshelf and makes a space for it. Turning back, he says, "The first thing that's clear, is that I'm going to have to take another look at the Ascension mess. I've been working as if the force of my will could accomplish the Lord's work." Charles pulls his chair toe to toe with Sam and sits. He speaks in a confidential tone. "I feel a bit like I did in my encounter with the thug outside Seven-Eleven. Strangely excited. Sunday, we sang a Song of Ascent for the Second Epiphany when I've never given any thought to what Second Epiphany is." The bishop asks, "What's happening?"

Sam echoes him. But Charles hears that Sam's "What's happening!" is said the enthusiastic way kids greet one another, in encouragement.

"The day before Bill Clinton and Al Gore are to be inaugurated to serve this country," Charles says, "you and I must address our reconfirmation of a duty we share, to be of service to that Other Country, the unseen world of spirit."

"Were you born in '37?" Sam asks. He feels prompted to share something with Charles known only to himself and The Seventy.

"Yes."

"For what it's worth, according to Pike, that makes you a member of the dreamcoat tribe, the tribe of Joseph. He would say you have been assigned the Fourteenth Injunction."

"The Fourteenth?" Charles asks, not comprehending Sam's

meaning.

"That's Paul's command to run the race expecting victory, in order to win the EL, the crown of Eternal Light."

"So," the bishop asks, "which injunction has your name on it?"

"The third." Sam repeats it, "Judge nothing before its time."

Charles Sprockett reaches over and puts his hands on Sam's knees. "I thank you, and I thank God, that I've been given this opportunity to know you better. Sam, would you give me your blessing?"

"Thank you, God," Sam begins, "for softening the heart of your servant Charles . . ."

21

Swear to God

Thursday, February 11, 1993

"Can I help you?" Francine calls to a young woman wearing a cheerleading uniform. The girl seems to be wandering in the hallway outside the All Souls' office.

The teenager raises a poster. "I'm looking for a bulletin board where I can post this notice. Our school is staging a musical."

"Which school?" the secretary asks.

"San Marino High, five miles up the boulevard," the girl says stepping into the doorway. "This is the church where my aunt goes. I wanted, like, to surprise her."

Francine gets up. "We don't ordinarily promote non-church activities, but if you speak with the rector, I'm sure he'll be glad to post it for you."

"Oh, I don't want to bother him."

"Oh, no bother," Francine insists. She brings the girl inside and knocks on Sam's sliding glass door. "Which musical?"

Sam slides the door open.

"*Bye Bye, Birdy.* My boyfriend is playing Birdy. He looks just like Elvis on the stamp, too."

"Lucky you," Sam says. The girl is staring at him, taking the measure of this handsome man against her preconceived notion of what the pastor of her aunt's church would be like.

Sam extends his hand. "I'm Father Garland, but I ask people to call me Sam." Although the girl returns the handshake, she says her name so softly Sam doesn't catch it.

Francine doesn't miss a beat. "Evelyn would like to put a picture of her boyfriend up for her aunt to see. Have I got that right?"

Evelyn shakes her head, no. "Actually, Jimmy's picture isn't on the poster. Just our names." She turns the 16 by 20 poster around and hands it to Sam.

"You're playing the Ann Margaret character?" he asks, leading Evelyn out of the office toward the gathering area inside the main doors of the church. "I saw the movie, what was it, twenty-five years ago?"

The girl smiles shyly. "About the time you left Olympus?" Sam cocks his head to look at her. "To me, you look like Zeus lost on his way home to dinner," Evelyn offers.

"Oh," Sam rumples the silvering curls above his left ear, wishing he could think of a rejoinder. "Thanks. Does Jimmy Mendoza *sound* like Elvis?" he asks as he finds an empty place on the kiosk for Evelyn's poster.

"Sort of. The thing is, Elvis died on Jimmy's birthday, when he was just a year old. So he feels a kind of special connection to the King. I think it's Madonna's birthday, too."

Sam feels his knees sag. He steadies himself against the kiosk. "And I suppose Jimmy was born in Memphis?"

"No, it's not *that* romantic. Denver, I think. Colorado, anyway," Evelyn says. "But Jimmy's mom has the biggest collection of original Elvis records you ever saw. Jimmy can lip sync them perfect. Of course, he'll be singing in the show."

"Why don't you bring some tickets around?" Sam says. It feels as if there isn't any air left in his lungs to say more.

The delighted Evelyn thanks him and shows herself out. She promises to come back again, with tickets. According to the poster, two tickets will cost $22. That's the price, Sam is sure, of seeing the son that got away. *Dear God. How many Hispanic boys named James can there be who celebrated their first birthday in Denver the day Elvis died?*

Sam pets the poster.

Back in his office, he looks through the phone book. Without Sharon's husband's name, his search is inconclusive. *It doesn't matter.* In the back of his mind, Sam hatches a plan. He decides he will wait until opening night to share this discovery with Bliss. Her daily prayers for Jimmy's safety have, in part, delivered him to her very doorstep, just as her persistent faith delivered her from the wrath of her bishop.

* * *

Sunday, February 14, 1993

Since Monday afternoon (when Peter White received a letter from the Office of the Bishop), there's been a sign posted on the door of Ascension's charcoal chapel:

BRING YOUR OWN CHAIR
9:45 A.M. SUNDAY
TO THE ASCENSION STOREFRONT OFFICE
THREE BLOCKS EAST
FOR OUR SPECIAL VALENTINE'S DAY
CELEBRATION OF THE EUCHARIST
WITH OUR OWN VICAR,
THE REV. BLISS BIRCH-GARLAND,
OFFICIATING
BY ORDER OF THE BISHOP.
—*PETER WHITE, WARDEN*

Bliss is radiant. Members and friends of Church of the Ascension have shown up in force. More than a hundred. "First, let me explain my name. You saw Birch-Garland on the notice Peter posted. That's the way it will appear in a ruling from the provincial court of appeals sometime next week. The bishop kindly decided to lift my suspension without being ordered to do so."

Applause breaks out, punctuated by shouts of greeting.

"When Sam and I were married, I suggested we try the hyphenated name. He was reluctant. He thought people might think he was trying to ride the coattails of his father-in-law. I was anxious to *stop* being seen as my father's daughter. I used Birch-Garland until after ordination, even though my driver's licenses never knew me that way. I hadn't taken Sam's name officially. Now, I've decided to pick it up again, even as we pick up the pieces of the work we have yet to do together."

"Yes," cry out several voices.

"Thanks. We're all grateful for the bishop's change of heart. I see Elizabeth Sparks is worshipping with us today. Welcome.

Please join us in making Bishop Sprockett a large valentine after the service. And, it's good to see Carolyn Banting again." Bliss nods in the direction of the reporter. "Some of you first learned of the plight of this congregation through her pieces in the *L.A. Times*. Feel free to speak with her. She's interested in featuring us once again when the appeals ruling is announced.

"Okay. Let's look at today's lesson from the book of James. James is said to have been Jesus' brother and a leading light in the church established in Jerusalem. It's easy to see he was a hard liner, a Jew at heart. He wants to preach about the commandment that says, 'Don't take the name of the Lord, your God, in vain.' He doesn't want us to swear. James gets so particular about the need to demonstrate your good works, that Martin Luther, who preached the importance of faith alone, actually ripped this book out of the bibles he came across, if you can imagine.

"James knows that when we're embroiled in a troublesome matter, it's tempting to let off steam. We might consider it harmless to swear on such an occasion, but he says, No. Reconsider. Pray instead. Some people swear without thinking, when they're overjoyed. James says, give it some thought. Sing instead.

"But, surely, if I was suffering great pain, I might be forgiven if I were to exorcise my agony by swearing? James says, 'Don't do it. Call in the elders and the wise healers instead. Have them pray with you.' Get the idea? James wants positive action as proof of faith. He respects demonstrated faithfulness to the oldest commandment on the books. He believes that Yahweh, God, requires it. He's heard the cover stories, the excuses we invent to hide our laziness. He knows how easy it can be to make an expletive of Yahweh/God, Jesus/Christ, or the Adonai/Lord instead of holding the divine name sacred. 'Don't do it,' he admonishes. 'Rather, confess your weaknesses and fears to one another.' We might say, see a counselor.

"But what if I've been deeply wronged? What if a bishop or a corporate executive, a bank official or a congressman fails to respond to my complaint? Shouldn't I be able to use God's name in condemning those bureaucrats whose idiocy complicates my life? Such fools have earned the strongest damnation. 'No,' says James. 'You won't be any better for grumbling or damning those who wrong you. 'Turn,' he says, 'to the prophets. Read them. And, *before* you lose patience, read the Bible with your friends.'

"The five things James recommends in place of swearing will build us up as people: prayer, song, calling for help, confession and scripture. And built up, we can resist the temptation to let disquieted thinking take hold. When I misuse God's name, I push the sacred away. Evil is all too happy to rush in. I'm approaching a subject that's a favorite of mine, the difference between making a bargain with life and making a commitment to the Creator of Life. In the first instance, we agree to go along, but only halfheartedly, 'until you fail me, God.' But when we make a commitment, we agree to go along until *we* fail. The phrase, 'until we are parted by death' is used in the marriage service to signal a commitment that's expected to take one to the grave. It addresses the literal, physical failure to be alive with another. But when we acknowledge God's supremacy, we're committed 'until we are united by death.' The hope of glory is the hope that divinity will live through us, not simply when we get to heaven, but even before we are united by death.

"In many ways, not just legally, our parish, Church of the Ascension, has died. Look around you, here today, we've been united in that death. We're going to rise again. The mystery of the One whose commitment is, 'I am with you always,' is that neither death nor immortality can separate us from Christ's love, borne on the wings of Wisdom since the first cosmic dawn and carried in the genetic memory of the human race. And while James asks us to separate from that which keeps us from experiencing our real needs, we're assured that our deepest needs, whether we can express them or not, are already known to God, our Father and, as Henry van Dyke pointed out, our Mother. And so, may the blessings of God, our Rock and Hiding Place, rest upon you this day. Now, and forever. Amen."

* * *

Peter White is kneeling, helping people tape their individual greetings onto the bishop's butcher-paper valentine. He's surrounded by crayon-wielding children who are adding a rainbow-scallop design and various symbols.

"Could I give you a hand?" Carolyn Banting says, offering to help Peter up. She wants to have a conversation.

"I saw you taking notes. Was this your first time to hear Bliss preach?"

"The second," Carolyn says. "Do you know, is it certain the ruling coming down is going to be in Bliss's favor?"

Peter answers obliquely. "Was South Central looted when the King verdict was announced?" That was news, he seems to imply. "What's certain is that Sprockett is reinstating her regardless. That's worth writing home about." Peter gestures to the valentine. "Don't you want to add something?"

Carolyn opens her notebook. She hands it to Peter so he can read what she was scribbling while Bliss preached:

> Life, for most of us, doesn't boil down to obeying a single simple commandment. If only it did. I come to church because I want what good people want: world peace and social justice. What am I offered? The chance to stop swearing. Strangely, Bliss Birch (Garland?) is able to make me see something new in that antique message. And I'm not sorry I came. This woman is a leader like . . . who? Her stance of powerful gentleness is as compelling as that of any man who can act from a gentle powerfulness.

"Beautiful," Peter says.

"Would you like to tape it on?"

Peter is surprised. "You, you don't want to keep it?"

"I'm in the business of giving away my words, remember?"

"But I just thought you might . . ."

"I might forget how to respond to perfection?"

Peter looks at the mulatto-skinned woman. She's the picture of perfection herself. Slightly masculine-looking in a casual, but not inexpensive, brown leather suit. A plaid blouse. She brings the '60s to mind. Peter was in high school when Kennedy was killed, too young to hit the road for Woodstock. His college generation hadn't heard of partying together over spring break. There was a basketball player, a year older, that Peter admired. Had these same chocolate arms.

"Don't be so long between visits," Peter says. "May I?" He's ready to remove the passage from Carolyn's notebook and put it on the bishop's valentine.

"Go ahead." Carolyn feels the shift. She can scarcely believe it's sexual tension, because she would've said she's never been attracted to a man. But just this minute, she wishes she could touch him. If there is fire here, even a casual gesture wouldn't come off as accidental. She reaches for the page and deliberately brushes

Peter's hand as well. "I should probably sign it first."

Peter doesn't draw back. The moment is extended. Without any effort and as slowly as if they are dancing, Peter bends forward so that, with only the smallest expense of energy, he gives her a hug and she receives it, as she takes back the notebook. It isn't dramatic. To anyone watching, it would look as if he were passing her The Peace.

It doesn't, however, look that way to Gabriel Luna. From across the room, he notices the embrace. He's never spoken of the life he's dreamed of leading, someday, with this man the courts made his guardian. And now, his face must not give him away. He turns on his heel to find himself looking into Sister's gaze.

"When you love somebody," she says, taking him by the shoulders, "you appreciate the way they move, and the way they move on. Don't be disappointed by change, Gabe."

22

Onion Rings for a Child Prodigy

Thursday, March 11, 1993

//My mom remembers Lawrence Welk's saying, 'Pea on your toes, Poys,' to his band," Evelyn Hernandez giggles. She and Sam Garland are trading stories about watching television. Evelyn listens attentively. The minister insisted on buying two tickets as a surprise gift for her aunt after she gave him freebie comps for dress rehearsal.

Sam, always comfortable chatting with people in his glass office—designed so he could talk privately with people while remaining in full view—enjoys the enthusiasm of this teen. She will be a good ally if it happens that her boyfriend is the same Elvis impersonator Sam regards as his lost son. Although it hasn't been confirmed that her "Jimmy" is the "James" Sam and Bliss adopted, Sam is persuaded by the circumstantial evidence. He'll *know* if Sharon shows up at the theatre. She was a remarkably mature high school dropout when she came to work as James' nanny. There would be no mistaking her.

"When I was fourteen," Sam says, having established that Evelyn will be fourteen next month, "I hitchhiked to L.A. from Oakland. While I was down here that summer, I came out to where your high school is now. I just wanted to stand there, because a month before, the place had been the scene of a tragedy. The first I'd ever witnessed on television. A live broadcast, like when people saw Jack Ruby shoot Lee Harvey Oswald. Except this one was about a little girl. Cathy something. Fiscus, maybe. She'd fallen into a well, and they had a camera at the scene. Live. Reporters were covering the rescue effort around the clock. It lasted more than a day. We were told Cathy's family was watching, too, until the descriptions became so sad they'd simply turned off the set and waited for the final word."

"I never heard about that," Evelyn says.

"Well, little Cathy was dead. But television had come alive in a terrifying way. Instead of being mostly for entertainment, it was for information and for connecting with the pain of the world. Tragedy brought strangers together. I'm not sure I would have come to L.A. just to see the Hollywoodland sign or to watch the Stars play at Gilmore Field. But, a child I'd never met drew me here."

"Did the sign really say Hollywoodland, back then?"

"Yes." Sam pulls open a drawer and lifts out a photo album. "Sounds like a theme park, doesn't it? Where do you think Disney got the tag for his playground?" Sam hands Evelyn a postcard from the album. It shows the old sign.

"It looks kinda sad," Evelyn says. "And, you know, that's how it is. Hollywood, I mean. My folks took me once on our way to the beach. I mean, we drove out Sunset and came back on Hollywood Boulevard. I never saw so many drifters and dopers. The panhandlers come right up to your car when you stop at the red lights. My dad said some of those kids make money by selling their bodies. Isn't that sick?"

"It's too bad," Sam says. "They don't have homes and families to love them. I know about that. I lived in foster homes from the time I was three. One after another."

"What happened?" Evelyn asks.

"My mother couldn't keep it together after my father died. When I told you I came to L.A. in 1949, I was really saying that was the summer I finally ran away from home. I was one of those street kids. Except, I didn't sell my body," Sam adds.

"You're an orphan?" Although Evelyn asks, her tone suggests the minister doesn't have to answer.

"I've been on my own for so long it feels that way. I definitely have a soft spot in my heart for children that get off to a tough start." Sam decides to open the door a little further. "When I was older, I was able to adopt a boy myself. Well, my wife and I did."

"I bet you're a great father," Evelyn says.

Sam doesn't want to explain it. "I like to think so," he says.

"I'm sure. You're easy to talk to, and you can remember the unknown stuff. I hope you and your wife can join our folks and us after the dress, for a little late night refreshment."

"We'd love to," Sam says. It's all coming together.

* * *

Thursday, March 25, 1993

The season of heat inversions is ahead. An evening much like this one will sign in on a scarlet, smog-assisted sunset. Tonight, however, there are only promises of rain. More rain. Since the unexpected deluges of January, Nature's watery intrigue has spelled disaster for home after home perched too close to the edge of the ever-popular, ocean-view hillsides. Freeway news, so often the lead story in this part of the world, has been bumped. Firemen giving evacuation notices ("Take what you can!") and collapsed or collapsing dwellings ("Bemoan that insurance coverage is not available here!") are spotlighted.

Sam and Bliss are going out. Amateur theatre. A film would be their more typical choice. In fact, Bliss has put together a Saturday evening video series, A Taste Of Heaven, for Lent at Ascension's storefront. She's showing *It's A Wonderful Life, Mr. Destiny, Almost An Angel, Ghost, Always, Heaven Can Wait* and *Field of Dreams*. Gabriel Luna suggested the series as a way to raise money to send his Menudo friend, Rodriguez, to the first national summit of gang leaders in Kansas City. It's going to be held on the first anniversary of the Rodney King verdict. *Ghost* attracted twenty street kids last week at two dollars apiece.

"I haven't told you," Sam confesses as they climb into the car, "exactly why I picked San Marino's *Bye Bye Birdy* production." It's only thirty minutes until curtain time. "The boy playing Birdy is named Jimmy. Coincidentally, his first birthday was celebrated the day the King died."

"You've seen him?"

"No. But I've met his girlfriend. I wanted to prepare you for the possibility that we'll meet his parents."

Bliss struggles to sort out her feelings. "I wouldn't get my hopes up. With thousands of babies born each day, a James here and there is to be expected."

"This Jimmy was born in Denver." Sam looks at his wife. He feels short of breath. She looks pained. "I think it's James, Beeb. Our James," he says. Then unexpected sobs come unbidden. Bliss leans over and puts her arm around Sam's shoulder. "I need to do this, Bliss. But if *you'd* rather not . . ."

She lays a finger on his lips to stop the thought. "Don't be silly. Whither thou goest, I will go," she says quietly.

* * *

Sam is grateful, going for coffee after the show, that Bliss can speak without embellishment. Evelyn and Jimmy are regaling everyone with an account of the last-minute dilemmas—dropped lines, missed cues, props that didn't show up. Bliss has revealed just enough concerning who she and Sam are: friends of the family. Though she has an advantage, she doesn't press it.

Sam is squeezing Sharon Mendoza's hand. *Everything will be all right,* he'd like to say. And finally he manages to say it. "Everything will be all right."

Bliss tells James, "When you were a baby, you and your mother lived with us for a time. Your mother was our housekeeper. My husband is the one, in fact, who suggested your name."

"James was the name of a bishop I liked," Sam says.

"Father Sam was an orphan," Evelyn adds.

Roberto, Jimmy's dad, picks up the thread. "I came from a broken home. That's why it was important to find a way to keep my family together. Son, you did us all proud tonight. Your mother, she thinks you have the most beautiful voice in the world. I gotta agree."

"You gotta be sincere," Jimmy jokes, quoting from his Elvis number that brings down the house.

Maintaining confidences usually comes easily to Sam, but it's difficult here. He'd rather not hold anything back, but Sharon's grip tells him she isn't ready to explain to her son that she gave him up at birth. Bliss keeps that part of the story to herself, sharing only what everyone can handle. She demonstrates that kindness must intersect with that truth that is told in love. Sam is impressed. She can pick up in the middle, without insisting, as he would, upon a recounting of the past. This evening belongs to the kids, after all.

Sam shares his onion rings with anyone who wants one. Leaning close to Sharon, he says, "I've known ever since Evelyn came with the poster that I'd be seeing you. But I didn't tell Bliss until we were on our way. Isn't she beautiful."

"She is. And you aren't so bad yourself."

23

The Tides of March

Friday, March 26, 1993

*A*ndrea Marvin reaches deep into the zippered section of her purse to produce three hundred dollars in cash. Five fifties and five tens. That's the fee for a psychic consultation with Ramson. This guy doesn't take plastic or checks. As for the $115 hotel bill? Andrea explains to the amiable clerk that, if possible, she'll put that on MasterCard.

"That's fine, Ms. Marvin," the balding gentleman says. He's handling hotel check-in as well as registration for the private Ramson appointments.

Over lunch, Andrea cancelled the rest of her day's appointments and phoned the Beverly Hills Hotel to pre-book an individual session with Ramson. She added the indulgence, overnight accommodation. If she wants to, the soft-spoken clerk reminds her, she may stay for tomorrow's group session. "The morning is included with your private audience fee," he says, repeating what was in Ramson's ad in today's paper.

At the moment, Andrea knows only that she's decided to meet Ramson. Having paid her money, she'll be regressed by him. He's the most notorious medicine man working the pop psych circuit in California's prestigious locales. For a few years, he hosted a call-in radio program, but Ramson is now a man of mystery detached from the professional community.

"Would you prefer to see him in his suite or your room?" the clerk asks once Andrea's signed for her room tab.

Isn't that the way, Andrea muses. Everything about connecting with Ramson requires spontaneous decision-making and impetuous action. That's part of his appeal. You hear about a spate of consultations he's given, often with celebrities. Then he seems to disappear into thin air until his next advertisement surfaces. Always you're invited to make an appointment "tonight." Andrea has no special regard for Ramson's gifts. She's simply curious. In the past, she's speculated it's a case of his going on alcoholic binges on the Mexican Riviera, to resurface when his supply of money, or easy women, runs low. Professional courtesy has kept her from airing these speculations, though some of his former students have intimated as much and more in journal articles. But little has been written concerning his actual practices. The man himself doesn't publish. He has no reputation to polish, no bridge to academia. He's a free spirit who trusts the public to pay more for his time than they would have to if they worked with someone local, someone like Andrea Marvin. In the end, one question may have peaked Andrea's interest. Is his charisma overpriced?

"Oh. I'll go to his suite," Andrea decides. She's surprised by her own tone of voice. It sounds as if she's an old hand at visiting men in their rooms. The clerk shows no concern.

Matter-of-factly, he says, "Ramson will call you about quarter to seven and decide when he can see you. Many people find it's better to wait to eat until after they've met with him," he adds. "Fasting, many times improves the experience of regression. The physical deprivation. It helps heighten spiritual perception. Or, so they say. Will you be needing any help with your luggage, Ms. Marvin?"

Andrea chuckles. "Luggage?" Her purse is almost as big as her overnight case and she won't be needing any help with either. "No. No, thank you, Mister . . .?"

"Levison."

"Mr. Levison. Thank you. This is all I have."

"Turn left off the elevator on the second floor," Mr. Levison says. He hands her a key. "Or use the stairs. Your actual room number is this," he points to it on his copy of her receipt. "We number your key otherwise for added security."

Andrea notices three sixes on a paper label affixed to her key.

"That's my spiel. But you're smart enough to see we've gone a bit further. All Ramson clients receive this 666 code." He lifts the edge of a label on another key. "You can remove this label if you'd rather not be recognized as his client. You . . . well, Ms. Marvin, to be perfectly frank, you don't remind me of *one of them*. This man triggers a chemical reaction in certain types. You'll understand what I'm saying when you see the others tomorrow. No offence. They kind of look alike."

The balding Mr. Levison shuts up. There's a sheepish look in his eye. He's either said much more than he meant to, or precisely that. Either way, Andrea is intrigued.

"I guess I'll be staying for the morning session," she says. The clerk smiles. "Good. And have a good evening."

* * *

"It's open. Come in," a baritone voice calls from inside the penthouse to which Andrea's been summoned. It's 6:55 p.m., the time for her appointment, as arranged only minutes ago in a brief phone conversation.

"My, aren't we the cautious one," the voice continues as Andrea steps into the living area. "So conservative, my dear. How will I get through to you in the little time we have?"

Andrea glances down at herself. She's wearing a dark blue linen blazer and skirt combination. The jacket swings open to reveal what she considers a daring accompaniment, a lace teddy with ruffles down the front. And, for added comfort, she's come braless. "This is risqué. I must have taken inspiration from Madonna to come like this." *Letting my guard down already?*

"I've seen Madonna. But now you, you are wanting what?"

Andrea finds it difficult to reply. The energies she senses in the room are baffling. Part of what she wants, is to know why.

"I'll close the drapes," Ramson says. But before he gets to it, he asks, "Would you care to look out?"

"Yes."

This is definitely a man who needs no second name. Like Cher or Sting, Queen or Rambo, Ramson has both a fearsome external fire and a winsome inner glow. He carries himself like a man in his thirties, but he has the presence of someone who's acquired the wisdom which only comes with age.

Andrea takes in the view, the city bathed in a haze of lengthening light dotted by splashes of neon. Although the penthouse of this historic hotel is situated only four floors up, its placement is singular for capturing the scenic afterthoughts of rush hour. Such splendor must come with a price tag to match.

"You paid to look at Los Angeles?" Ramson finally asks, putting a hand against Andrea's back.

She doesn't get defensive, but breathes in the scene even deeper. "I'm a psychologist," she says, "familiar with hypnosis. I don't think you'll have any trouble taking me back."

"Yes, of course, *back*." Ramson reaches to close the drape. "For a moment, I thought you might be the one from this group who would ask to be progressed. The future, you know, can be very stunning. Beautiful. Much like yourself." Ramson's compliment seems genuine. Andrea doesn't resist it. He isn't needy. He isn't the shyster she was prepared to fend off.

"You have confidence, do you, that the future can be entered?"

"There was a time," Ramson says, taking a seat and tipping his head back, "when all we had forgotten *was* the future."

Andrea finds herself giving Ramson a compliment. "You're even more compelling in person than your reputation makes you out to be."

"Improving with age, I guess."

Andrea realizes she can't tell within thirty years how old Ramson might be. The thought is disturbing. *Am I chasing a rainbow?* "Am I in a time warp?" she asks.

"Not you. Not you, my dear. No. Sit down." Ramson gestures toward a comfortable chair. "Unless you would prefer the bed."

"A chair is fine."

The chair seems to be expecting her body. The fabric is neither cold nor hot. The seat cushions her perfectly, allowing her arms to rest comfortably in her lap.

"Are we ready, then?" Ramson asks.

Andrea closes her eyes.

"Do you see those two doors in front of you?" he asks.

Andrea is surprised. No long induction? No swinging pendulum? "Well, yes, I do see them," she answers.

"Which one will you go through this evening?"

As she sees them, the one is black with the word PAST appearing on it in white letters. The other is awash in color with a dark FUTURE printed on it. "I will go through the one that opens to me," Andrea answers.

"Good. You'll find that to be the choice you've always understood as the best," Ramson says.

Andrea sees herself strolling on a beach. Shortly, she recognizes the scene. It's a favorite haunt of hers at Laguna. Although she remembers she's responding to hypnotic suggestion, the sound of gulls, the smell of seaweed, and the feel of sand between her toes are palpable. Pleasantly so. The sun is about to set. A few clouds amplify the amber gold. The waves continue to lap, lap, in a steady rhythm.

"What's that on the horizon?" Ramson asks.

Andrea welcomes his question. "Which horizon?"

"Look to the side of the sun, where you'd expect a sun dog," Ramson suggests. As he speaks, three hundred and sixty degrees of horizon come into Andrea's view. Far to the west, a fleck of red appears to catch fire. It gains momentum, rising like a ship's sail to conquer the curvature of the earth: a horse's head. Then, atop the horse which is galloping, galloping on a mirror of ocean beneath its hooves, a figure. Impossible. As it approaches, Andrea sees the rider more clearly, a delicate Japanese woman. Her porcelain features contrast with the black fire of the animal. She is wrapped in a scarlet cloak of dappled brocade, almost a kimono. It trails behind her and the speeding steed for miles, billowing up into the heavens where it is claimed by the sky.

Finally, the creature slows down. Brocade settles beneath its hooves, and the porcelain figure sits as if on a breathing platform, but close to the crimson waves. In the clouds behind her, four figures take shape. Sumo wrestlers. The first is garbed in a white mawashi; the second is sporting a red sumo belt. The third wrestler's girth is defined by a black mawashi; the last wears a gold girdle.

"Look to either side," Ramson instructs.

Andrea sees a fur-covered Eskimo to her right, whether man or woman she can't tell. The figure is accompanied by four graceful polar bears which circle in a slow-motion dance. From the south, on her left, a donkey brings an old woman forward. She clutches a dark sack against her body. Five members of her party walk along beside her. Andrea sees an older man, a woman clothed in blue who may be the man's wife, and three children.

"Who are they?" she asks.

"In due course." With Ramson's answer comes the sound of wings. It's more commotion than a few seagulls would raise. Behind her, Andreas senses thousands and thousands of birds preparing to land. Their wings chop the air like the rotors of a helicopter.

From among the birds comes a voice. "Thank you so much for all your help." Andrea turns. It's Sam Garland. He and Bliss are standing together. With them is a Latino boy Andrea doesn't recognize. "We found our son," Sam says. Andrea doesn't know it, but she'll hear Sam say this very thing next Monday night.

"Turn full circle a few times, slowly," Ramson suggests, "then, when you're ready, find yourself back in this comfortable room with me." He waits several minutes.

When Andrea opens her eyes, she asks, "Was that the past or the future?"

Ramson smiles. "It was, as I saw it, the present to the fourteenth power or, what is sometimes labeled too carelessly, Eternity."

"And what's the point?" Andrea asks. "What does it mean?"

Ramson stands and goes to the window. He opens the linen draperies. Only the embers of a sunset remain. He leans against the sill and reaching under the edge of his v-neck shirt, he lifts a necklace Andrea hadn't noticed. He drops his head to remove it. The glass-like beads catch the last light in an intriguing way.

"It means, come," he says. "This is for you." He seems to collect the light from the night. The necklace, a crystal mountain, is cradled in the palm of his huge left hand. "Would you like it?"

Andrea gets up. "Of course."

"On this day, the last Friday of the first month on the old calendar, I repeat a promise that was made to me forty-two generations ago, 'Return to me, and I will return to you.'" He slips the necklace over Andrea's head and brushes each of her cheeks with a kiss.

"Goodness," she says. It isn't just the unexpected weight of the garland that surprises her, but the way in which, almost magically, she can see Ramson and herself in a new light.

"Come and look in the mirror," he suggests. "If I stand behind you, our auras will merge. Less distracting." He raises his hands high over their heads. "What do you see out here?" he asks.

"A band of red," Andrea says. "Translucent, but crimson."

Ramson moves his outstretched hands downward, looking like Leonardo's exemplar of the man of perfect proportion. "Just as the rainbow is seen, red at the uppermost, outermost and bottom-most. But, what do we have here?" Ramson asks repositioning his hands in the fourth band. It's sandwiched in the middle of seven Andrea can see.

"Green."

"Yes. That indicates a healing-in-progress or, at times, the reverse: heart troubles. It depends upon the client. Understand?" He can see she doesn't. "You'll get accustomed to watching for it. Physical, emotional and spiritual heart trouble manifests visibly in this midrange. And, this?" He moves his hands into the yellow and then the orange light. "This orange range is about reproduction, the sexual spectrum. Look closely, here," he points to a fuzzy spot, hip high on Andrea's left side, "the quest for a partner. And you'll find other life pattern correspondences. Put your hands here." He positions Andrea's palms high in the blue light. "This is the communication channel. As we follow yours down into the egg of light encasing you, notice how the blue becomes paler. The further we go from your throat, the less vitality. What does that say?"

Andrea can only guess. "I'm not into counseling mothers?"

"Or you've had difficulty speaking to attract a lover. Perhaps he's not embodied at this time." He pats her back gently.

Ramson moves to sit in the chair Andrea occupied during the session. He closes his eyes and, for a moment, Andrea supposes it is a signal for her to take her leave. "Don't go. You'd like to hear what this vision of yours means, would you not?"

"Yes." Andrea is intrigued by a change in tone and demeanor in Ramson. As she sits in the other chair, he doesn't open his eyes. His speech is more labored as he says, "This woman arriving on horseback in the red gown is you, in the future. And the bodyguards are your priests, in this life. You, it also is, in the past, playing as the Eskimo child and her bears do. And Anna, the old grandmother, coming back from Egypt by burro with her daughter Mary, the son-in-law Joseph, Jesus and the girls. This, we can tell you, so you will understand, is a community memory. It is not entirely your own."

Ramson opens his eyes. "The birds are your way of giving power to the vision. This final image holds much in common with my own power vision. That's the reason for the gift I've given you. I don't make a habit of that. I mean, I didn't know I was going to part with it. Another time, on a spiritual plane, you'll see the fulfillment of the vocation you've begun reclaiming in this life."

"But what does one *do* with a power vision?" Andrea asks.

"My dear. My dear. You return to it, and it will return to you. You enter it, and it enters you." Ramson is creating a dance with his hands as he speaks. "Give it away, and it will give you away. Hold it down, when you would be held back. Let it have its freedom and so, reclaim yours. Do you play tennis?"

"Not since high school."

"The most important thing in improving one's tennis game is always to do only what you're able to do. In match play, if you try to do more, you'll be shown up as less of a player. It's the same with a power vision. Do with it just what you're able to do, and never try to do more."

"And, the reason you've given me your crystals?"

Ramson extends a hand, as if asking to hold his necklace one last time. Andrea doesn't hesitate to remove it. He lays the circlet across his knees. "Tomorrow, I suspect the real world will land on you with a thud. These beads are a remembrance, a gentle reminder that this evening happened. I was here, with you, for this once-in-a-lifetime experience. And the beads remember that."

Tears have welled-up in Andrea's eyes. "Thank you," she chokes.

"What is it you'd still like to ask?"

Andrea's mind empties itself of question after question which she *doesn't* need answered: Will I find a marriage partner? Are you an angel? How will this evening affect the rest of my life? My practice? Am I really going to use that crazy aura stuff?

She remains silent.

Ramson smiles. "Blest are those who have not seen, and yet believe. But you, you my dear, have seen. I'm sure the Second Coming is going to make a difference to us all, at least as much as the first one did."

The two sit together in silence.

Ramson finally speaks. "If you'd like a chakra massage before you go, just stretch out. The floor, or the bed. Face down to start."

Andrea chooses the floor. She's expecting to feel Ramson's hands, like a back rub. What a surprise when she receives only an etheric touch. Without his leaving his chair, Ramson washes his energy into hers, deeply. She feels her body starting to levitate. In an inner ear, she hears him joke, "Mr. Levison would be proud of you." As she lets that thought go, she senses that by morning she'll have forgotten this feeling. She'll say, "I was borne on angels' wings," but she won't be able to recall the how of it. Ramson is lifting her to a place where memory is foreclosed. To wake up here would be to know one's immortality. "Do only what you can," Ramson gently reminds her as they step beyond time.

Moments later, as he brings his beloved back from the silent, cleansing journey, Ramson kisses the beads and whispers, "Set me as a seal upon your heart."

"Where was I?"

"With me."

Andrea is ready to go. She takes the necklace and excuses herself. "I love you," the crystals sing into her fingers.

"I love you," Andrea says quietly. She pats the temporary 666 affixed to Ramson's door as she closes it. Now she understands. She has an engraved invitation to meet him anytime, in spirit, if she can figure out *how* one accomplishes that.

"And, I love you." *This must be the listening Sam Garland does.*

* * *

Ramson, dressed all in white, faces a roomful of paying guests. He stands beside the podium on a platform that runs almost the length of the ballroom. Two wide aisles have been carved into a sea of chairs from the entrance doors on the wall opposite the stage. Nearly every seat is taken.

"Thank you for coming," Ramson says to five hundred people who were invited here only yesterday morning. "The first thing I'd like to address is the question of who will be attending this afternoon's Master Class. If those of you who'd like to attend would open your notebooks, we'll see what magnets are in place today."

Andrea has no idea what's going on. She assumed this morning's session *was* a master class. Where have all these students, or groupies of Ramson's, come from?

"All right." Ramson positions himself beside an overhead projector. "I'm ready." He switches the projector on and writes the date. "How many of you have a Taurus sun, moon or ascendant?" he asks. Several hands go up. "Count yourself out of this first question, please," he says, switching off the projector. In a moment he announces, "I've begun receiving. Let those who connect with this energy translate the message they receive."

Andrea flips to a blank page in her Daytimer, but writes nothing. Glancing around, she sees that nearly everyone near her is writing. She watches as one, then another, puts down their pen. Ramson takes a seat in a blue brocade-covered chair at the rear of the dais. Then Andrea notices that a young man a few rows behind her, far to her left, is standing.

Ramson gets up and comes to the fixed microphone even though he's wearing a body mike. "What have you written?" he asks the young man.

"My opening sentence, in fact all that I wrote, says, 'a boy tenth from the end of the next to the last row.'"

Ramson smiles. "You did a little calculating and discovered that that was you?" he says lightly.

"Yes."

"Good." Ramson switches the overhead on. He's covered the bottom two-thirds of his transparency, but at the very top, he's written, "a boy, 10th from the end of the next to the last row." There is a round of applause. "Would you join me, please? And any of the rest of you who match after this point, please come up as well."

Ramson lifts the cover from the rest of the page. It is completely blank. There's an audible gasp from the audience.

"What is it?" Andrea asks the woman seated beside her.

"Blank. It's never happened before," the lady says.

Ramson intones his response. "This is a refreshing change, wouldn't you say? Any of you non-Taurusites who wrote nothing in the first experiment are welcome to join this afternoon's Master Class. Where are you?" No one stands up.

"That's you," the woman beside Andrea says.

"Oh, I don't know. I don't think . . ."

"Stand up," she insists. "You wrote nothing. Get up."

"Anyone?" Ramson looks around.

"Here," the woman seated by Andrea calls out, jabbing her on the shoulder.

"Of course, Ms. Marvin," Ramson says. "You may stay where you are. We'll see you this afternoon, one o'clock, at my penthouse? Please. Now, let's see how many of the rest of you our young man from the next to the last row can draw? Remember, this activity is not in any way competitive. Your time will come—when it should, perfectly. And in order. But, I remind you, doubling isn't a parlor game. Don't try this at home." His remark sparks a roar of laughter. "Matching any receiver is unlikely. And it certainly isn't necessary. Whatever you have written has value. So relax. Maybe you're here to experience what will come, even in the very *last* moment of our official time together this morning. Before the buffet."

Andrea remembers that the price for this three-hour session is only ten dollars, but twenty-five if you opted to stay for lunch. The entire event is included in the $300 she parted with yesterday. She finds her mind wandering. Did anyone else in the room *have* a private session yesterday, she wonders. She saw just two keys, after all, with the 666 label.

Ramson resumes his seat. Young Ten-from-the-End steps to the projector and switches it off. He knows the routine. After putting Ramson's overlay and his own corresponding page into a folder marked PROOFS, he pulls a fresh plastic overlay from its box. He leans to the microphone and says, "I'm ready to receive."

Several people open their notebooks and begin writing.

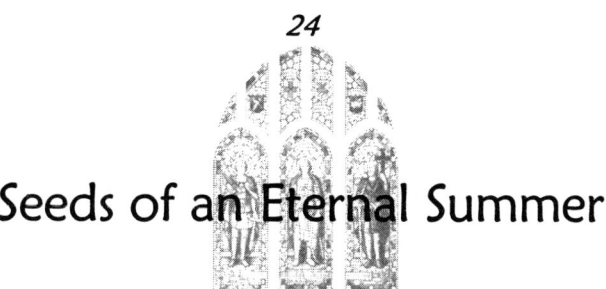

24

Seeds of an Eternal Summer

Monday, June 28, 1993

//Have you visited Tomorrowland?" Andrea Marvin asks Bliss and Sam. They nod. Disneyland dates are a Birch-Garland tradition, done in May, either to celebrate their anniversary or Sam's birthday. He turned fifty-eight on the 31st of last month, and cancelled his appointment with Andrea that evening so he and Bliss could have the entire day to themselves in Anaheim. "Well, I propose to take you someplace similar tonight, a Tomorrowland of sorts. But more personal. I've been guided there frequently myself lately." The idea of introducing her clergy clients to Ramson's progression technique was Andrea's.

Sam interrupts. "Does this involve hypnosis?" He knows Andrea has participated in several weekend master classes since March. He thinks they've involved her being hypnotized.

"I prefer to employ creative visualization. We can induce a past life or future life vision, using relaxation. So, no, I *won't* be hypnotizing you. It won't be like those old horror pictures," Andrea swings any imaginary pendulum. "You'll be free to counter any suggestions I give. In fact, you and your deep, knowing self will be in control of everything. The Universe is so generous. You're not going to believe it. I mean I was overwhelmed. A person can pick up *any* loose end. Even a casual curiosity. Anything that's ready for resolution. We can address physical pain, but often it's a piece of emotional or mental garbage that's just sitting there waiting to be hauled away. You'll be surprised."

Bliss is already surprised that Andrea has so much to say. "Sounds intriguing. I'm ready."

Sam nods and Andrea begins.

"Close your eyes, then, and let me continue making suggestions. We won't consider them hypnotic suggestions, just gentle prods—not unlike what the better angels of your nature would ask of you." Andrea's voice is smooth and continuous. She makes an upward tour through the body, suggesting release to any tensions of the day residing in feet, knees, thighs, belly, heart and lungs, lips and throat, or eyes. As she makes this scan, she asks her clients to seek out the loose ends, the residue clinging to emotionally charged relationships. What pain is tucked away in the unexamined recesses of consciousness?

Sam recalls that going into the pantry this morning, he was taken off guard by a thought of Effie, Andrea's deceased bird. The pantry seemed like a cage. Pouring over his collection of tapes, Sam had lost the will to get on with it. He spent a long time thinking of the bird and, also, of course, of Andrea. Try as he might to leave such sentiments alone, his feelings for her catch him off guard.

Bliss finds herself replaying Gabriel Luna's decision to make restitution of several thousand dollars to his former street gang. It resulted in Menudo's pitching in with Ascension's festival. They helped erect a donated carnival tent.

"Whatever comes to mind," Andrea says, "is being processed in the Universal imagination. From there, we catch wind of the reality we've chosen to explore. Where love is, there will be no loose ends. See yourself, now, moving in the direction of a phone booth. And when you've stepped into it, lift the fingers of one hand to signal that you can see the dialing pad."

Andrea doesn't have to wait long for her clients' signal.

"Your inner knower has selected coordinates you're going to dial. This phone booth isn't ordinary. It's a vehicle. When you step out of it, you'll be in whatever space and time you need to visit, in order to tie up any loose ends that presently concern you. So, as you're ready, see yourself dialing. But also, return the receiver to its cradle." Andrea takes several deep breaths. "Turn now and come out of the booth, taking all the time you need to explore this territory and to speak with whomever is present. Know that when it's time, I'll bring you back to this booth and you will return easily to your present reality."

"Stepping out takes more energy than I realized," Sam thinks, though he has no trouble. Although he can recognize himself, Sam knows immediately he isn't going by the name Sam Garland here.

He's come to Tokyo. By what means? An inner voice suggests, *by use of the molecular redistribution principle as practiced for millennia by elect adepts in the hidden monasteries.*

Then, in a breath, Sam knows himself as Kiyodayu. Kiyo has a place as a son, in the Shikimori family. The males of this household oversee the refereeing of Grand Sumo. It seems to Sam that he's interviewing himself to get his bearings.

"I, Kiyo, have been elected for a promotion. I'm to referee Juryo division bouts now. My uncle's reaching the mandatory retirement age, 65. That triggers my advance. How fortunate that I am with Miko again before reporting to the work tomorrow. Miko can walk on my back to massage my muscles, so I am prepared in body and spirit for these new duties on the dohyo.

"She tends carefully to the kimonos I wear in the ring." Sam notices, as he speaks of her, that Miko is a Japanese version of Andrea. The realization nearly breaks his reverie. But Miko steps forward bearing the silk kimono he's to wear tomorrow. The intricacies of the pattern are absorbing. This, too, has been handed down for centuries. The new kimono is floor-length. Miko produces the tabi, the split-toed white socks, required for juryo-rank referees. She has thought of everything. She leads him to where she has laid a fine, elaborate fan, the prop he'll use in announcing each victorious wrestler. By gesturing to the corner, east or west, from which the victor entered, he will, at some future time as Kiyo, Sam realizes, have the privilege of sealing judgment.

Miko's measured steps bespeak the ancient discipline she chooses. For everyone knows that to be a traditional Japanese woman these days, is outrageously old-fashioned. For the sake of their Shinto religion, however, and the peace of mind afforded by simple customs, Kiyo and Miko are pledged to the path of a traditional life.

Andrea is asking her clients to return to the phone booth. "Dial home," she suggests. Then she waits. After both clients have opened their eyes, she asks, "Anything of interest there?"

"Oh, my," Sam says. "I think I jumped ahead a couple hundred years. Though maybe it was back. Your having said Tomorrowland may have run some interference on me."

Bliss is surprised. "My loose ends must be closer. I was standing at what seemed to be the deathbed of Rodriguez, the leader of Menudo. I knew, in the visualization somehow, that he's been suffering with HIV. That isn't even anything I actually suspect."

Sam has questions. "Isn't this just imagination? I haven't looked at a future that's actually going to be. I've looked at a possibility my mind projected."

"Did it feel real?" Andrea asks.

"It did," Sam admits. "And I seemed to know particulars of something I have no experience with."

"What was that?" Bliss asks.

"Refereeing sumo matches."

Bliss laughs. "Well, why not? You and Charles Sprockett."

"But, will it happen?" Sam asks Andrea.

"Or," Andrea reminds him, "has it already happened? Is remembering it, all we have to do in order to heal history? Regression helps me see a larger canvas. And perhaps I *can* change a future I'd like to avoid."

Sam reflects. "My vision was like a dream. And, it doesn't seem *impossible* that a dream created when the imagination is in high gear, might come true."

"Bliss?" Andrea says. She wants to keep a balance.

"When I see myself beside Rodriguez's deathbed, I don't think the challenge is for me to get ready to assist AIDS victims in particular. But it's a warning. I'm on the verge of having to get along without a person who helped me get this far. I think it's saying I'm not going have my father to lean on much longer. Or the fence around our undercroft, which Rodriguez helped us build, *is* finally going to come down."

"Good," Andrea says. "There's no right or wrong way to interpret a dream; no right or wrong way to set about incorporating a vision of the future. But the effort helps us make a request we didn't realize was ours to make."

"Which is?" Sam asks.

"An opportunity to take all the time we need. Another day."

"Other avenues," Bliss adds. "Options."

For Andrea, those words confirm a prophecy Ramson penned for her on the occasion of what she felt was to be their last consultation: "Be patient, dear one. We have all the time we need to discover one thing: that Love is stronger than Death."